A Bird in the Hand

A Year in Cherrybrook

Book Three: Autumn

CHARLOTTE BROTHERS

I dedicate this book to my cousins. A couple of you unknowingly influenced a few details of the story. Thanks for being the fun and clever batch you are!

Contents

Chapter One

October, 1838

Christopher Morton angled his tall frame low in the seat of Lord Stafford's coach so that he could more easily see the local passing countryside. If all went well, he and his mother would soon be calling this corner of Dorset "home". There were waving swaths of golden grasses against small forests of orange-clad trees and evergreens. Now and again, herds of grazing deer or livestock lifted their heads, shook their ears and turned their backs to the biting autumn air.

Wind rocked the carriage and Christopher tried to relax the tension in his body, and sway with the movement of the box rather than fight against it. What would be, would be, he reminded himself. No amount of vexing over his forthcoming meeting with the Earl would change the outcome.

Christopher was not particularly given to nervousness (which he was most grateful for today), having inherited his mother's quiet steadiness. Indeed, he was so much like his mother that he hardly knew what looks or proclivities he might have inherited from his father, having never met him. His mother refused to speak of his father, although her refusal was always offered with a small smile, as if she recalled happy memories and not dismal ones. She appeared completely without malice for the man who had abandoned her with a small son and a handsome annual allowance.

He looked on with increased interest as the pastoral view began turning up farms and houses much closer together. They were entering a town. The village did not appear to be a large one, but it was bustling with activity. As they passed through the centre, Christopher saw the usual mix of farmers and tradesmen with a few well-dressed gentlemen and gentlewomen with children in tow. After a few starts and stops, they continued along what he perceived as the main road which led off in a westerly direction. Soon he spotted a tall, narrow church spire and, as they drew nearer, he observed the church had a graveyard behind it, and a large vicarage beside it. The home and church were separated by a row of ancient apple trees and spindly lilac bushes dressed now in yellow. Christopher wondered if they might turn into the circle drive, but no. The driver did not slow the horses.

Before leaving the village completely, Christopher saw an imposing stone manor house and a stable set well behind a low, moss-covered stone wall. There was a footpath from the house which crossed the road and emptied into a fallow field with a fine willow copse at the heart of it.

Soon this pleasant country aspect became a second town, and this time the carriage did slow to a stop. After leaning down to smile at Christopher and rap upon the glass, the driver jabbed a finger in the direction of a church nestled back, well away from the road. This must be it! Saint Joseph's Church! Bending forward to better see out the window, Christopher observed the church's strong Norman exterior and low, broad tower-shaped steeple. There was a grassy-edged stream winding on the south side of it, and a quaint, wooden footbridge that connected the church yard to the grounds of a solid-looking house that looked like an overgrown cottage. That must be the vicarage. It was impossible to see it clearly, even though many of the trees were bare, but it appeared to be constructed out of the same stone as the church with simple lines and a tall chimney at each end of the main house.

Christopher sat back a little as the carriage lurched forward once more, carrying him onward to Penfield House, the residence of Lord Stafford, the Earl of Wellsey. It was the Earl who had summoned him here. Christopher had been informed by letter that the current vicar of Wellsey was approaching his eightieth year and, quite understandably, wished to retire to his daughter's home. The Earl was seeking a replacement.

The carriage made a couple of turns, then passed under an ivy-covered stone arch and onto a private drive lined with tall hedges. Finally, they reached the clearing in the centre, and Christopher caught his breath at the beauty of the home and grounds. Penfield House was grand in the old style, a not-unpleasant blend of architectural eras unified by the consistent use of pale stone. It sprawled across a well-tended lawn, with a walled garden, orchard, and forest beyond it. While he watched, a pair of red-haired footmen exited the house and stood, waiting, as the conveyance which bore him slowed to a halt.

Once stopped, Christopher Morton emerged from the carriage, and with a grateful nod and word of thanks to the driver, turned to face the pair of young footmen, who promptly led him up the massive stone steps and into the house.

The front hall was as grand as any to be found in a country residence of its class. The high-ceilinged room was furnished with costly carpets, oversized porcelain vases on marble-topped tables, and family portraits. The portraits seemed particularly fine, and Christopher might have stopped to study them, according to his interest, but a starchy manservant stepped to his side, and cleared his throat meaningfully.

"Mr. Morton, sir?" inquired the man as he bowed, and ushered Christopher down a long hall.

At the end of it, Christopher was waved through a pair of double doors and into a well-lit gallery as the servant announced, "Mr. Morton, milord," and spun on his heels, returning in the direction from which they had come. Christopher stood in awe just inside the doorway. While the front hall had been impressive, it was nothing compared to this!

"Do not stand on the threshold when the lord invites you in," called a gruff voice, raspy with infirmity. This pronouncement was followed by a violent cough, and Christopher quickly spotted a bent-shouldered, yet elegant man sitting at a carved mahogany writing table in a far corner of the enormous room. It was an inspiring but draughty-looking makeshift study. As Christopher bowed and approached, the gentleman leaned forward, resting his elbows heavily upon the desk. "You can say 'lord' with a small 'l' or a capital one and the saying will still hold true. At least I hope I will find it to be so when my time comes to approach Heaven." Here the Earl chuckled drily.

Christopher smiled cautiously, "I trust so, indeed, milord."

Christopher squinted at Lord Stafford to take his measure and at the same time accepted the same scrutiny of his own person. The Earl, a pale man, dressed in black, was perilously thin, yet Christopher could see that his eyes were sharp and his features well-formed. He was like a shadow holding fast to a large handkerchief. Not wishing to offend Lord Stafford by staring, Christopher blinked and turned his attention from his host to his host's art collection. The paintings on the walls formed a patchwork of splendour, hung in loosely defined rows from floor to ceiling. As a student in Town, he had relished every opportunity to visit the galleries and museums that he could, but pieces of this quality were completely unexpected in such an out of the way place as Wellsey. This was incredible.

"Go ahead. Look around," the Earl invited him. He sounded pleased that Christopher had taken such an obvious interest.

The subjects of the works varied. The Earl (and assumedly his predecessors) had excellent taste, thought Christopher. Everywhere were classical landscapes and some very new, fresh-looking landscapes of England, as well as several masterfully painted portraits. There were paintings of hunting dogs and hunting scenes spotted with deer and partridges, and a pair of small religious pieces with fine colouring.

When Christopher had taken his fill, he turned with some embarrassment to Lord Stafford and began to apologise for his rudeness, when his words were swept away, mid-air, by the bony hand of the Earl.

"Do you enter service for want of money?" demanded his lordship. His face wore a shrewd look, showing he was very much aware of the harsh honesty of what he asked.

"I do not want for money. My mother and I are well provided for. However-" Christopher took a step forward, "I wish to be beforehand with you, my lord, I am not a gentleman with a name, and do not wish to spend my days idle, doing good for none but myself without a place or occupation. I believe I have nothing to lose by serving others and contributing something to my own family's upkeep."

"Are you married, then?"

"No, sir."

"Ah, you wish to be."

Christopher's mouth turned up just a touch at this. "Not yet, sir. I have not yet met the lady."

There was a long pause during which the Earl stared unblinkingly at him, and with such critical intensity that Christopher could hear himself swallow nervously. He stood tall but shifted his weight slightly. Where were the rest of the questions that surely were to be put to him? Christopher waited expectantly.

Lord Stafford was overtaken by another long coughing spasm and Christopher winced uncomfortably to see it. When the Earl had recovered the use of his voice, he asked, "You will begin in January?"

Christopher stared in astonishment.

"That is all, my lord? You have no further questions?"

"I asked you if you would come in January. That is my final question, our interview is over. Do you accept my offer?"

"With all due honour, I do accept. Yes! Thank you, milord!" Christopher's eyes widened at the dry wit and caprice of Lord Stafford, and he nearly tripped over his own long legs in dizzy gratitude as he stepped closer.

The bent man leaned slightly forward in his chair and extended his hand. He took Christopher's hand in his, and clasped it firmly for just a moment.

"I like you, and that is a *very* good thing," growled the Earl. "It is more important to me than you know." Lord Stafford held up his handkerchief in anticipation of a cough, then slowly lowered it when no cough presented itself. He lifted his head wearily, but there was nothing weak about the set of his chin or the intensity of his gaze. "Do your utmost for the parishioners of St. Joseph's. Nourish their hearts. Educate them. Inspire them."

Christopher knew he beamed, and he could not stop the excitement in his voice, "You have my word, milord. I shall do my best!"

The Earl again lifted his handkerchief and held it to his mouth and said with finality, " I have no doubt you will. Now, good day to you." Having forced out these last words, he broke into a fit of coughing.

Christopher respectfully left the gallery, understanding that he was dismissed.

His mind was frothing with all that had just taken place, when he heard quick steps coming towards him down the hall, and he fixed his attention forward. A fashionably-dressed man, roughly his own age, rounded the corner ahead and swept dramatically into the hall. He was closely followed by a small, nearly bald, gesticulating servant, who was trying desperately to discourage him from his course.

The servant was a small man and had to hurry to match the long strides of the tall gentleman.

"... but, my lord," pleaded the servant, "your father expressly stated that he was not be disturbed! He is meeting with-" here the servant noticed Christopher and broke off. He dropped back, obviously relieved to be done with his chase, and panted breathlessly. "Never mind, milord. I see your father's guest is just leaving."

The Viscount lifted his chin a fraction and raised an eyebrow and languid eyelid at Christopher as they met in the hallway. He nodded as he swept by, saying in a somewhat threatening under voice, "I hope you have not put my father in a foul mood, for I am in no great humour myself."

Christopher stopped abruptly and turned to look back at the re-treating gentleman. The door had not yet shut when he heard the young man address his father caustically, "Miss Hamblin is a cold fish, sir. I have done as you required and have paid a call on Lord and Lady Hamblin, but I shall do no more today." There was a momentary pause, and then he heard the Viscount continue in raised tones, "And does the noose tighten? For I just met a chap in the hall! I can only assume he is Hamblin's nephew. Haven't set eyes on the fellow before so I wouldn't know…" Catching himself as an intruder upon a private conversation, Christopher continued to the front hall and the gin-ger-haired footmen (whom he decided must be brothers if not twins, they looked so alike) nodded to him, opened the door, and saw him out.

Christopher felt a sort of exaltation as the late October wind tugged at his hair and hat. He smiled at the grey sky and then at the coachman who put the steps down for him. Christopher stepped directly into the carriage and with a laugh waved to the driver who responded with a hearty smile and a nod.

"Congratulations, sir!" said the coachman observantly. He tipped his hat. "You must be the new vicar now, then?"

"I suppose I am, my good man. Thank you! I am pleased to say that my mother and I shall take up residence just after the Christ-mas holidays." Now that his first meeting with the Earl was finished, Christopher felt his stomach growl. Before closing the door of the coach behind him, he said to the driver with a grin, "Please, take me to an inn where I can get a good meal. I find that I am excessively hungry!"

Chapter Two

S everal months later...

It was indeed a beautiful painting.

Cherise stood very near the small oil painting that hung in the dark entry to Saint Joseph's Church and scrutinised it. Then, with a swift look to the left and right to be sure that no one was watching her, she bent down and stared up at the painting from one lower corner and then the other. From this unladylike position she could force the feeble sunlight to highlight the brush strokes, and understand something of how the artist had constructed this delight.

The painting depicted a popular biblical subject, the Descent from the Cross, but the skilful rendering of this piece was extraordinary! The edges were gracefully drawn, and the colours carefully shaped, each bit of drapery looking as though it were unblended with any colour outside the edge of its contour, and yet it had escaped the stiffness typical of that technique.

How wonderful to have even this small of a work, painted by an obvious master, here in the heart of Dorset! She knew the Earl was fond of art. Odd that before now he had not donated any paintings to the church, but she acknowledged that age could change the natural way of things. She had heard it whispered about that, because the Earl was in poor health, his only son had secretly purchased the piece, and had gifted it to the church under the directives of his father or, perhaps more interestingly, to impress him. For her part, Cherise was not convinced that the Viscount had anything to do with the matter, but any recollection of the Viscount brought with it a wave of anxiety, so she resolutely put Lord Penfield out of her mind for the present being and forcibly concentrated on the treasure before her.

Her recovered reverie was interrupted by the sound of energetic footsteps striking the stone slab walk just outside the church. Straightening up quickly as the door opened, she turned to see the silhouette of a tall and powerfully-built man halt abruptly in the shadow of the doorway.

"Excuse me madam for this intrusion," he said in a sonorous, yet gentle voice. "I will return later." Pausing and holding up a hand, he added, "Please, take your time and enjoy the art." And without giving her time to reply, he was gone.

Somewhat puzzled, Cherise stood still until she could no longer hear his footsteps, then she turned once more toward the painting. There could be no harm in staying a few more minutes. She sat upon a narrow bench and reverentially took her fill of the beautiful canvas. Satisfied, she rose with a contented sigh and turned to go.

Before she could slip out unobserved, she heard a different, much lighter set of footsteps, on the front stairs. The door creaked again on its ancient hinges, and Cherise blinked as a shaft of pale light entered through the opening door and shone directly into her eyes.

A woman entered. And, as she moved from the shadows into a patch of light shining down from a high, narrow window, Cherise could see that the lady's hand was extended in a friendly greeting.

"Hello! To whom do I owe this pleasure?" asked the woman.

She was taller than Cherise, and well dressed. Her clothing was not conspicuous in any way, yet the fabric was of a fine quality. She had curly hair of a rich, golden brown touched with silver, intelligent grey eyes and a generous mouth. She smiled charmingly at Cherise and seemed eager to make her acquaintance.

Cherise smiled cautiously and took the woman's offered hand, nodding politely. "I am Miss Cherise Hamblin. From Cherrybrook." She glanced behind her, "My mother is a great friend of Mrs. Terrence's. It was she who told us of the new painting."

"Hamblin. I am familiar with that name." A faint frown of concentration crossed the older lady's face and then she glanced up at the painting and said quickly, "Yes, we are fortunate indeed to have it." She smiled at Cherise. "I am Mrs. Morton, the minister's mother."

Here was Mrs. Morton! Cherise regarded the lady with increased curiosity, for she and her son had been the subject of several lively dinner conversations between her parents. Last September, her mother and father had put forward their nephew (her cousin), Stephen Hamblin, as a possible curate or vicar for the Wellsey parish. Without the honour of a discussion, the Earl had chosen instead to settle the living upon a complete stranger, Mr. Morton. It was a peculiar circumstance. Not only were her parents piqued by the Earl's perceived contrariety, it had made the Mortons fascinating subjects of local curiosity and much idle gossip.

Remembering her manners, Cherise returned her smile warmly and said, "I am very happy to make your acquaintance, ma'am. Turning back to the painting with a sweeping gesture, she asked, "Please. Would you tell me what you know of this?"

Pride lit the woman's face. "It is a jewel, is it not? It is from a lesser-known Venetian painter or studio, we think. Its origin can really only be deduced by its style. My son says the grace of it assumes that at least the faces and a portion of the figures of the grieving Mary, the Magdalene, and of course, Christ himself, would have been painted or personally overseen by a studio maestro. Or maybe those portions that are especially masterful were done by a talented young studio painter, who later developed a name that we might recognise if we were ever to learn it?" She sighed. "So many questions and too few answers. I sympathise. At any rate, it is a tremendous gift."

"Does no one know who gave it to you?" Cherise queried.

With a slight smile, Mrs. Morton replied, "I believe that the person or couple wished to remain publicly unacknowledged."

Mrs. Morton's eyes grew wide as an idea struck her. "Miss Hamblin, would you like to have tea with me?" She paused, flushed slightly, and continued. "That is, if you have the time. I do not wish to be too pressing."

"I would very much enjoy that," Cherise refrained from adding, *and perhaps meet your mysterious son*? "My mother accompanied me, but she has no special interest in art." Cherise's gaze flicked to the painting and back again. "She is with Mrs. Terrence until half past eleven. I am to meet her there."

"Lovely," replied Mrs. Morton with a smile. "We shall have just one cup and then I see you must be going. Either myself or my son will escort you to meet your mother when you feel it is time."

Mrs. Morton's footfalls on the stone floor echoed about the empty church as she made her way back to the door. After one last glance at the admired painting, Cherise followed her, walking quickly to catch up.

Outside, there was a cold mist where the warming earth met the cool wind. There were still broad, shallow puddles, and soft earth. Tender grass and crocuses stood up amongst the old growth, greening the grounds beside the road and footpath.

Mrs. Morton led Cherise down a gravel walk toward the footbridge that led to the house. While they walked, they talked about painting. Cherise was thrilled to discover her companion might be nearly as well-informed on the subject of art as she was herself.

When they reached the middle of the footbridge, they paused to enjoy the view. The water burbled as it hurried the spring rain down the stream to meet the river. Cherise had always loved this little bridge and shapely waterway, and although it had been many years since she had played here as a girl, she recalled those halcyon days with fondness. They resumed their walk to the vicarage along the old path, both sides of which were planted with bulbs and early budding bushes.

"I have always admired this riverside garden," confided Cherise, "and it looks as though you are preparing to improve upon it?" She gestured in the direction of freshly dug earth and piles of stones.

"Oh, yes. My son has enjoyed drawing out maps of well-established plants, and reflecting upon possible alterations. 'Although beautiful, it is an old garden,' he says, 'and wants for fresh design'."

"Here we are, then! Come in!" invited Mrs. Morton when they reached the front door of the manse. When Cherise had used the boot scraper and had been ushered inside, she looked around, wondering if she might find Mr. Morton. When she heard only the light voices of women, likely in the kitchen, she sighed inwardly, but soon she was absorbed by Mrs. Morton's tour.

She slowly walked around the outside edge of the parlour in which they were to take tea. It was a cosy room, with lots of warm pinks and deep reds worked into the cushions, wallcoverings, and carpets. There were ornate lamps everywhere, many books and some small, tabletop sculptures as well as many framed drawings and paintings. The room was bursting with what Cherise considered 'approachable pictures', florals, natura morte, as well as some portraits. An elegant, longcase clock ticked out the minutes near the entry. Cherise stopped in front of the fireplace to look at several small, unframed drawings which were leaned up on the mantel willy-nilly, some bending over a little as the paper had curled in the humidity. There were drawings of wild mushrooms, a couple of sketched water eddies, wildflowers, tree bark; all were highly-detailed nature studies, expertly done.

"Are they not lovely?" asked Mrs. Morton behind her.

"They are indeed,' answered Cherise, turning round with her hands clasped innocently behind her back.

Mrs. Morton tilted her head slightly to one side and asked, "Do you draw, Miss Hamblin?"

"Only in the service of painting the drawings afterward," answered Cherise ruefully. "I get very impatient with the weather this time each spring, for I cannot wait to be out of doors with my paint box again. In the winter I study, and do copies, but everything comes out so frightfully dull, colourless unless I have my painting practically pressed against a window," she laughed.

"Oh yes, our fine English weather gives us all cause to complain, does it not?" smiled Mrs. Morton. She took a few steps toward the bell pull. "I imagine there are many fine places to paint around Cherrybrook and Wellsey. Christopher and I enjoy long country walks." She heaved a sigh. "For the time being, we are kept to the roads because of the wet ground and mud. He is the one who enjoys drawing, however." She lifted her brows as she rang the bell. "Your father is Lord Hamblin?"

A housemaid curtseyed in the doorway and Mrs. Morton asked for tea for two.

Only for two. Mr. Morton would *not* be joining them.

Coming back to the conversation, Cherise responded, "He is, yes. We Hamblins are an old family here. The Hamblins and the inhabitants of Penfield House have lived as neighbours for generations."

Mrs. Morton settled back in the delicate padded chair, and put her fingertips together. Saying with a sort of smile, "Lord Stafford is much older than you are, but I suppose his son might have been a playmate of sorts, or is perhaps now a suitor of yours. Ah! Here is our tea." Turning to speak to the serving woman, an older, round-faced robust woman near fifty, Mrs. Morton said, "Thank you Thea. I shall pour. You may come and fetch the tray in half an hour." Mrs. Morton motioned for Cherise to join her at the small, round table.

Cherise was very glad that Mrs. Morton had not asked directly if the Viscount was a suitor. The note had been offered as a statement and not a question, and it seemed that the lady really had no intention of prying after all, for the rest of the conversation was about the usual small subjects, such as what did her family sponsor by way of holiday festivities? Were there any annual events that both Wellsey and Cherrybrook planned together?

"We hold two dances nearly every year," replied Cherise, smoothing her skirts with one hand as she sat down. "One at Christmas and the other for any occasion that might merit one." She held out her hand to accept a saucer and cup of tea and continued. "The fighting has eased in Spain, we hear, and many of our soldiers are coming home. If they should make their way here in the next few weeks, as they are anticipated to be, I am sure we will arrange a ball in their honour. I do hope that we will have no cause for sorrow! Although in many ways my parents are very like others, they are generous, and never forbade me from associating with Cherrybrook's well-established families." Cherise flashed a smile at her hostess. "I am personally acquainted with a few of the soldiers and should be greatly saddened by any loss." Mrs. Morton neither looked shocked nor dismayed by this, but rather pleased.

"And you, Mrs. Morton, you are no relation to anyone in Wellsey? For that is what I have heard. What do you think of such a country life?" Cherise scooted ever so slightly toward the edge of her chair to hear the lady's answer.

Mrs. Morton smiled serenely, "When I was a young woman, I had my season in Town and met Christopher's father there, but I never cared for the society of most of the fashionable set, so was comfortable to return to the country. And as you see, I do not want for domestic comforts."

Cherise noticed the sparse detail given to the lady's marriage and subsequent child. Her husband had obviously been *somebody* to have situated her so well. Cherise lifted her chin and looked all around the room approvingly. "It is a lovely house, but surely to have fine tastes, and to be confined to rural life…"

"Tell me, Miss Hamblin," said Mrs. Morton with a quizzical smile, "do you find *your* life in Cherrybrook more confining than comforting? I cannot take your measure in this. You must tell me."

The question was direct, but Cherise preferred such shocking honesty to gentle fictions. She took a deep breath and said, "I shall confide in you, ma'am. I am passionate about art, and the reason I came today was because I am starved for the want of it!" Mrs. Morton lifted her eyebrows questioningly, but did not interrupt. Cherise went on, "But I will say that if my life could stay the same in significant ways, yet allow me to see more of the world and the paintings that I have only read about in books, I could be happy remaining here."

Mrs. Morton took a final sip of tea and her eyes crinkled in a smile as she looked over the top of her cup. "The Viscount is now in Paris, I believe."

Cherise let that comment fall and lie untouched. She did not want to voice her private opinion of Lord Robert Penfield, Lord Stafford's heir.

A short time later, both ladies had finished their tea and the chiming of the clock announced that it was three-quarters past the hour. Mrs. Morton rose and walked to the window and leaned forward to look off to the right in the direction of the church and then turned, saying with a note of disappointment, "What a pity. I was trusting that my son would be home before now to meet you and return you to your mother. But never mind, I shall accompany you instead."

"Oh, Mrs. Morton, no. It is completely unnecessary, I will be fine on my own, I am--"

"Heavens, child, it is no trouble. I shall not pay a visit to Mrs. Terrence unannounced, but I will see you to her door."

There was nothing to do but accept. Mrs. Morton was as determined, apparently, as Cherise's own mother.

As they crossed the bridge and angled off to the left instead of toward the church, Cherise made sure her companion did not see her steal one last furtive look for the elusive Mr. Morton before leaving the grounds.

Once they reached the home of Mr. and Mrs. Terrence, Cherise thanked Mrs. Morton again for the impromptu tea, and they parted ways.

No sooner had Cherise been delivered to the ladies in the parlour and had greeted Mrs. Terrence, when her mother informed her that it was time they were on their way home. This plan was amenable to Cherise, who found her mind still quite occupied with her teatime conversation. While her mother and Mrs. Terrence exchanged parting civilities, Cherise walked slowly around the room. She paused at the large window that faced the street and looked off in the direction of the church. She could just barely make out the form of Mrs. Morton, and it looked as though she had stopped to talk to a man, but they were too far away for Cherise to see his features.

After having left Miss Hamblin in the care of Mrs. Terrence's footman, Mrs. Morton spotted her son on the street. "Christopher!" she called out.

She hurried to his side and he turned to welcome her with a smile.

"Mother! I am pleased to see you here, but I thought you were occupied at home?"

"I was, but now I have just come from the Terrences' front door."

"You were calling on Mrs. Terrence?" asked Christopher in surprise.

"No," she replied smugly. "I invited the young lady you discovered in the church this morning home for tea, and have just accompanied her back to her mother, an especial friend of Mrs. Terrence's." Mrs. Morton glanced behind her, eyes shining. "The girl happened to be Miss Hamblin, daughter of the Cherrybook squire and his lady!"

"Is that so?" Christopher's finely-shaped eyebrows rose with interest, and a smile played at the corner of his lips.

"Yes," said his mother. "And I quite like her!"

"Tell me, would you describe her as 'a cold fish'?" he asked, eyes twinkling.

"Mrs. Morton stared at her son, shocked. "Merciful Heavens, no. Whoever said such a thing?" Without giving him time to answer, she went on, "Not you, you would have told me about meeting her if you had. I am convinced of it."

"Really?" said Christopher with teasing interest. "Well, it may be that you shared tea with that miserable, damp creature, the intended bride of Lord Penfield."

Mrs. Morton pulled her face long and waved her hand at him in mock protest. "I sincerely hope not, for she is far more interesting than he is." She walked beside her son, her hands behind her back.

She looked at him sideways, "A cold fish did someone call her? Most assuredly, not," she said emphatically. They took a few more steps in comfortable silence. "You ought to have stopped home to be introduced."

He grinned generously. "I thought perhaps to leave her to you. Anyway, it proved to be a good decision. I shouldn't want to be accused of poaching a lady from the Viscount's pond."

Mrs. Morton smiled a little and looked off beyond his shoulder before replying, "You are very clever with your contexts, Christopher, but I wish sometimes you would be serious." She gave a ladylike harumph, but wore her firm, pleasant, but enigmatic expression. Christopher had learned long ago that when she was in such a mood it was best to change the subject. Nothing would be gained by argument.

Chapter Three

Although Cherise made two more visits to see the small Deposition painting, she did not happen upon the vicar, nor his charming mother.

The days grew warmer and the spring sun brought flowers and trees into bloom. Whenever she could, Cherise took her watercolour set with her to do some painting out-of-doors. Although she sometimes chose to distract a servant from their duties and have them come along as a companion, there were a couple of places on their land she was able to safely visit alone: the garden (because it was in the shadow of the house) and the willow copse at Carter's Pond (because it was so nearby, and no one else wandered there).

One fine day, Cherise entered the morning room in full expectation of a refreshing and larger than usual breakfast. She planned to haul her colours to the garden to paint, and did not want to be plagued by hunger once she had set up her folding stool and had gotten out her colours and water jar.

Her mother was seated at the writing desk with an opened letter spread out before her and a smile upon her face. She looked up distractedly when Cherise came in.

"Good morning, my dear," greeted Mrs. Hamblin. "Sit and sip your chocolate while I tell you what Mrs. Terrence has written to me."

Cherise helped herself to a large currant bun and a plate of eggs, then in one graceful movement, melted into a chair to eat and listen.

Her mother took a deep breath and, lifting the letter, she read, "Louisa writes that Lord Penfield has installed new church pews, and they are much more elegant and comfortable than the old ones." She lowered the letter and leaned forward earnestly. "To me, such an action indicates a new sense of caring, of proper stewardship for the people of Wellsey, who rely on the Stafford family."

"It could also mean that Lord Penfield finds Mr. Morton's sermons tedious, and needs to make himself more comfortable," replied Cherise slyly.

"You mustn't speak such nonsense! And besides, my dear," her mother added censoriously, "it is quite unlike you. Remember that Lord Penfield is our superior in both fortune and station. If he has shown a decided preference for you, we can only be thankful for it."

A thoughtful, dreamy quality settled over Lady Hamlin's expression that set off an alarm in Cherise's chest. *She wasn't beginning this old song again, was she?* Before Cherise could warn her from it, her mother continued.

"You know how very much your father and I want to see you comfortably situated."

She knew only too well.

Lady Hamblin tilted her head and said sweetly, "and the Earl finds you suitable."

"Does it matter to you that his son does *not* find me so?" Cherise reminded her.

"Do not be ridiculous, child. You were scarcely civil when the Viscount called the last time, poor boy. I felt quite sorry for him, struggling as he was to make conversation."

Cherise's eyes opened wide in disbelief. In her opinion, Penfield did not "make conversation." He talked and expected others to listen. But she refrained from argument and sat patiently as her mother went on.

"I implore you, my dear, give him a chance to prove himself. He may have changed! And do not forget that as his wife, you would have the opportunity to direct him." Here her mother fluttered the missive in her hand, " And you interrupted me before I got to the exciting part... Louisa says not only are the pews wonderfully comfortable but, you will appreciate *this*: there is work being done in the church apse! An anonymous donor, she says, has bespoke a stained-glass window from none other than William Holland!" Lady Hamblin lifted her eyebrows and looked pointedly at her daughter. "Anonymous donor? Nonsense! I cannot see how the donor could be any other than Lord Penfield. You see? With a father like the Earl, the son is bound to concern himself with art... eventually. Just as you must wish."

Cherise gave a derisive sniff and her mother looked at her sharply. Open disrespect was not part of Cherise's character (however she might be feeling inwardly) so she looked down at her plate and nodded her head enough to indicate filial acquiescence, but no more.

Her mother mused. "I cannot help wishing that the Earl had tried to exert himself a bit more to tame Lord Penfield when he was young, for then you might like him better. The boy took too much after his mother, a flighty, silly thing, and spoiled mothers often beget spoiled children, I say." With this pronouncement she resumed reading her letter.

"Louisa goes on to say that the Mortons are settled in nicely now, and the town is quite enthusiastic about them."

Cherise blinked slowly and toyed with her spoon. "I have met Mrs. Morton and she is a very genteel sort of woman. Remember? I told you about her. I asked you to call upon her afterwards, but you did not."

Almost as if Cherise had not spoken, her mother went on, "But it *was* rather a snub from Lord Stafford to refuse even to *meet* your cousin. Stephen would have made a very *economical* solution for Wellsey, but the Earl flatly refused! And then he brought in that complete stranger with a mother to support!" She sighed. "Mr. Morton. Such a young man to be chosen as a vicar. It was all exceedingly strange, in my opinion."

Cherise answered in a faintly strangled tone, "I am sure he and his mother are very kind and proper, Mother, and now you and Papa have been rude by not calling on the Mortons when they had first arrived. I am sure that when you are introduced, you will be pleasantly surprised by their fine manners; and afterwards, happily resigned to them being our neighbours."

Lady Hamblin thought for several moments before releasing a long sigh. "I am prepared to forgive them now, and you are right. I am sure that we have made a poor impression."

"I hope *I* did not," reminded Cherise gently.

"It is good that you, at least, did meet them."

"I met Mrs. Morton only, Mother. I have not met Mr. Morton."

Lady Hamblin brightened suddenly, "Well... you shall. We all shall!" She clapped her hands excitedly, "Young Mr. Trellaway, Lieutenant Trellaway now, and another officer, a friend of his named Captain someone-or-other-"

"Captain Fortescue," supplied Cherise.

"Captain Fortescue," continued her mother, "are returned from Spain, along with the Jennison boy and Andrews. I think we ought to organise a spring dance in their honour, and I will lose no time in extending an invitation to the Mortons. May I count on your help with the arrangements?"

"Yes, but before we start, I should like to finish my breakfast and go out. It looks to be a fine day and I intend to make the most of it."

"You will stay on the property, dearest?"

"Yes, if I am not in the garden I will be at the pond."

Lady Hamblin was already happily commencing to write a reply to Mrs. Terrence but looked up suddenly. "We can begin on invitations for the dance this afternoon?"

"Yes, Mother, if you wish it...."

"Very good, then," her mother replied, her eyes gleaming. "With luck, the Viscount will be home. I do hope he will attend. We must send word to him immediately that we are holding a dance."

Lady Hamblin and Cherise sent out invitations the following week, and set about organising the dance. There were to be summer wreaths and ribbons and the best musicians in the county. The pair of them, with the help of household servants, decorated the ballroom and kept receipts of all the letters of acceptance. The days passed quickly, and soon the evening of the dance arrived.

As preeminent members of Cherrybrook and hosts of the evening, Cherise and her parents now stood at the head of the room, receiving guests to what they proudly had named "The Soldiers' Ball".

As soon as Mr. Morton entered the room, Cherise spotted him. Doubtless, it was in part because he was exceedingly tall. But also his mother, whom she recognised, held on to his arm.

Mr. Morton was very handsome, more so than she had expected. No wonder the entire town of Wellsey was so taken with him! He was well formed, well dressed, and had wavy, light brown hair like his mother's, almost copper-coloured, that shone like burnished gold in the lamplight. The young vicar's gaze travelled deliberately around the room, coming to rest upon her, and Cherise's curiosity became significantly more piqued when she observed in his expression a blend of kindness, good-humour, and intelligence.

She could not stop herself from openly smiling at him. He returned her smile warmly and took a step toward her.

His mother, Mrs. Morton, released his arm and stopped to speak to an acquaintance, but Mr. Morton seemed to be moving toward Cherise as if drawn by a magnet. He glanced at her so often that he managed to stumble into Mr. Whyte, a short, stout man who gave a sharp cry of displeasure. Mr. Morton took a gentle hold of the older man's shoulder and must have made an agreeable apology, for by the end of it, Mr. Whyte was wreathed in smiles once more and was nodding agreeably, even taking Mr. Morton's hand and shaking it fervently. Afterwards, Mr. Morton seemed to change from his deliberate course and now stopped to speak with other guests.

When the crowd near her family had begun to dissipate, Cherise (who had been furtively watching Mr. Morton all along) observed that he and his mother had reunited and were, this time, quite determinedly making their way to the head of the room.

Cherise tried to breathe evenly, reminding herself that he was only a vicar.

He stepped up to bow and thank her father and mother first. His warm, baritone voice was as handsome as his person. Indeed, the sound of his voice had stuck in Cherise's memory from that day in the church. She listened attentively but tried not to stare. His mother remarked upon the kind invitation that brought them to Cherrybrook this evening.

Finally, it was Cherise's turn.

Mr. Morton turned to face her directly, and for one glorious second, he looked her steadily in the eyes. His were pale blue, and looking into them was like looking into the heart of a flame or a cloudless summer sky. There was nothing frightening in their depths like there was in some men, only a friendly sympathy. Mr. Morton blinked slowly and bowed; a hint of a smile played upon his lips. Cherise forced her attention back to her mother and Mrs. Morton, while her heart pounded fiercely.

"Mrs. Morton," Lady Hamblin inclined her head. "My daughter tells me that she has already made your acquaintance." Then, looking up at the son, she said, "And Mr. Morton, we are pleased to meet you at laaast..." She drew out that last word as if it had somehow been his fault that so much time had passed before their inevitable meeting.

Cherise shivered with annoyance. Lady Hamblin continued, "Now that summer is nearly upon us, introductions and visiting are more the thing, aren't they?" She smiled complacently. "I am sure our paths will cross again very soon. Oh, I am, of course, *Lady* Hamblin and this is our only child, *Miss* Hamblin."

Cherise blushed, which she *seldom* did. She could not decide if it was because of Mr. Morton's rapt attention upon her face, or whether it was the note of condescension in her mother's voice. If her mother had taken an unbiased look at the Mortons, she would have seen that they were the perfect combination of expensive clothing and genteel manners, with no airs of pretension.

Mr. Morton's mouth turned up quizzically on the sides, and he gave a little nod of comprehension as he addressed Lady Hamblin. "Ah, *Lord* and *Lady* Hamblin of Cherrybrook." He turned to Cherise once again and said, "*Miss* Hamblin." Then, inexplicably, he grinned as if something droll had suddenly occurred to him.

Cherise was unsure of how to respond at first, but then she remembered that his mother almost certainly would have told him about her having come in for tea. She let out her breath slowly and said, "I am pleased to finally make your acquaintance, Mr. Morton."

"No," he said, the arrested look still upon his face, "the pleasure is entirely mine."

Cherise felt a sudden, dizzy fascination which she had never felt before. There was no reasonable explanation for it, but it was as though the air between them snapped like a pinewood fire. At least, that is how Cherise felt. She had the strangest suspicion that he knew what she was feeling, and felt the same, and wordlessly had agreed to keep it secret. She believed she did well to remain properly detached and calm on the outside, but inwardly she was only too aware of the hammering of her heart.

Attempting to focus now on his mother, Cherise said, "Mrs. Morton, I am so pleased to see you again! I must tell you that I have come twice more to see the painting and crossed the bridge to see if you were home to visitors, but alas, you were out."

"Did you? I am exceedingly sorry I was not at home, Miss Hamblin. I very much enjoyed our teatime chat and I hope that we will have another such occasion soon," her gaze flicked briefly to Cherise's mother and she smiled a little sadly.

Since the introductions had been exchanged, and the requisite minutes (no more, no less) in the receiving line were spent, the Mortons moved off to the side of the dance floor. Cherise periodically glanced in their direction. She hoped no one noticed. After every guest had been greeted, she went about the room to attend to the comfort of their guests. The musicians took their places at the head of the room and began to warm up, playing snatches of popular tunes.

When the first dancers took to the floor, there was a small disturbance from the bottom of the set. Her friend, Miss Merritt, had unaccountably taken ill, and was helped from the floor by her dance partner, Captain Fortescue. The Merritt family took their leave immediately thereafter. Cherise danced the next dance with the distracted captain, followed by two reels with young men she had known since childhood days. She did not fail to notice that the vicar had not yet danced. Needing to rest her feet as the music started up once again, Cherise wove her way through the smiling dancers and onlookers towards the chairs that lined the side of the room. As she went, her gaze darted from one tall head to another in search of the vicar or his mother when she heard her name.

"Miss Hamblin." Mr. Morton had materialised behind her.

She turned, and her hand flew to her chest.

"I am sorry. I startled you," he said, talking over the hum of the crowd.

"You did not startle me," said Cherise, not entirely truthfully, also forced to raise her voice.

"I am glad to hear it," he replied. He hesitated and asked carefully, "You might stop clutching your gown, then?"

Cherise looked down. She had thoughtlessly grabbed at the top of her gown, near her heart, and to any onlooker it would look as though she was no less than terrified! With a small laugh, she quickly smoothed her dress front, then dropped her hands to her sides.

He did not leave her time to be embarrassed before he spoke again. "You look fully recovered, thankfully. I am here to invite you to dance. That is, if your card is not already full?" His eyes crinkled pleasantly at the corners. He seemed desirous for her to feel at ease in his company.

She smiled, "I have the next dance free. Does that suit you?"

"Indeed, it does," he grinned boyishly. I will be back directly, Miss Hamblin. Thank you," he said, bowing slowly before he moved away.

Cherise wondered if she looked as delighted as she felt.

The current dance was a long one but when it ended, Mr. Morton, as promised, reappeared to lead her by the gloved hand to the floor.

They were to perform a quadrille, a challenging dance, and it took great concentration. There was little opportunity to speak, but they smiled profusely in those moments when they faced each other and caught their breath together. By the end of it, Cherise was happy to have the excuse of appearing shaky from the dance, for she was fairly certain that the feelings of unsteadiness she was experiencing had begun the minute Mr. Morton had taken her hand, and had nothing whatsoever to do with the physical exertion of commanding her steps.

Once the music stopped, he guided her from the floor, and leant down near her ear and said, "I learned about you from my mother, as you might have guessed. However, I must allow your name is also familiar to me for a rather unfortunate reason, Miss Hamblin. I believe you have a male relation that shares your name who was put forward as a candidate for the parish that I am now humbly grateful to lead. I sincerely hope that he found an excellent situation elsewhere?" Mr. Morton's expression looked touchingly anxious.

Cherise glanced in the direction of her mother and then leaned closer before replying, as quietly as one could in a crowded room. "Thank you, no, not as of yet, Mr. Morton, but we anticipate he will soon. My father has more than a little influence in our part of the country, and perhaps by the time the year is out, my cousin will have a church and home."

"I do extend my apologies. I was sorry to learn that someone that you care for was inconvenienced on my account. Lord Stafford is an old and very dear friend of the Morton family, and it was kindness itself that, hearing of my preparation for the church, he communicated that when the former vicar retired, I would be offered a living."

"I am very happy for you, sir," she said as his eyes searched her face. Cherise smiled at his look of concern, and her brows lifted. "Truly, I am! You must believe me!" Desiring to change the subject, she asked, "And do you like your new home?"

"Oh, very much, I -" Here Mr. Morton was interrupted by an out of breath Lady Hamblin, who burst upon the earnest young couple.

"It is as hot as an oven, despite it only being May!" Mrs. Hamblin was fanning herself somewhat frantically as she came up beside Cherise, and gripped her by the wrist. "Cherise dear, I want you to come and greet the Viscount. He has only just arrived." Mrs. Hamblin then looked up, as if she had just noticed the vicar was standing in front of her, and said with a stiff smile, "Mr. Morton, you know Lord Penfield, of course? Perspective Earl of Wellsey?" she added pointedly. "But of course you do. How silly of me! Doubtless you have been introduced, for you must consider him and his father your benefactors."

Mr. Morton's face remained gentle but that bright light, which had lit his eyes moments prior, faded to a patient carefulness as he inclined his head politely to Lady Hamblin. Putting his hands behind his back, he followed his hostess's gaze to the entrance. "Oh, yes," he acknowledged. "I did not think he would return in time to attend tonight, but, ah! So he has." Then, with a sharp intake of breath and a smile, Mr. Morton turned to Cherise and said, "I thank you for the dance, Miss Hamblin. I hope we shall take another turn about the room at the next such occasion. Enjoy the rest of your evening." He bowed deeply to her and her mother, then disappeared into the crowd.

Cherise longed to stand thoughtlessly watching after him, but her mother, with a discreet guiding hand, propelled her toward the Earl's heir.

Lord Penfield, Cherise had long believed, was a self-important block who neglected others in conversation, and spoke mainly on three topics: his exalted position, his latest winnings, and his unerring judgement of horseflesh. Oh, yes. And he frequently abandoned his ailing father for long stretches of time. In short, she not only knew him to be uninteresting, she thought him unforgivable.

The Viscount had a quick smile. Too quick. And he blinked his eyes rapidly as he talked, rocking back and forth on his heels and looking about the room as he spoke, as if he were desperately on the lookout for someone else more interesting to talk to. It always made Cherise feel that she must be terribly dull, or it gave her an upset stomach. Tonight, the contrast between Mr. Morton and Lord Penfield managed to do both simultaneously.

"Ah-ha!" Lord Penfield said in greeting, "The charming Miss Hamblin." She thought he did not look very charmed. He sucked in through his teeth. "Always a pleasure, always a pleasure. How have you been? Holed up in Cherrybrook, still? Won't they give you a Season?"

Before she could reply that she had been in London much of last summer (*did he not remember that?*), he was rattling on ahead.

"I was thinking of you not so very long ago, actually." Here he paused for emphasis. "Yes, I really was! I was in Rome, at the Vatican, looking at art treasure after art treasure, and I thought of you back at home. I imagined how much you would have appreciated what I was seeing. Piece after grand piece, on a scale that you simply cannot imagine! I recalled how you enjoy painting, you see? Do you still get out much? To paint, that is?"

"I do. As often as I can while the weather holds. There is nothing like an English spring, all the trees are just that shade of green -" She broke off abruptly when her father walked up and the Viscount turned aside.

"Ah! There you are, Hamblin!" Lord Penfield said offhandedly. He tucked his chin and smiled indulgently. "Talking to your elegant daughter here, you see?"

Cherise smiled blandly at her father as he joined the conversation, which inexorably turned from art to horses.

It seemed like no time at all before she noticed Mr. Morton and his mother exchanging necessary civilities and moving toward the door. Her shoulders fell, and she tried to tell herself that it did not matter. She inched away from Lord Penfield and her father to speak with Miss Lyle and a couple of other young women she had grown up with. But once the Mortons had gone, it must be acknowledged that for her, the night had lost its chief, and perhaps only, attraction.

Chapter Four

Even though the vicarage was not large, Christopher had fallen in love with it immediately. There was the small winding, grassy-edged stream that dithered through the property, dividing the cottage from the church grounds. From the front of the house, one had to walk a fair way to reach the road. The portion nearest the road was meadow-like, a sunny place with a smattering of old fruit trees and berry bushes with tall grass, but near the vicarage, the plants were clustered close together, giving the home a nestled-in appearance.

If Mr. Morton needed to get his thoughts in order after a particularly trying day, he found that spending time outdoors cleared his mind admirably. He slowly walked along the border beds of the rectory garden, stooping now and again to remove a finished flower or pull an undesirable plant that had sneaked in amongst its neighbours. Christopher much preferred digging and discovery to such delicate tasks as flower care, and more often than he cared to admit, he forgot about domesticated plants altogether when he found something curious, such as a tawny toadstool, he had never before encountered. He was also selfish enough to conserve time for that greater pleasure:

drawing. An enthusiastic student of botany and design, he trudged for miles, and often stopped and sketched as he pleased. Having no enemies (at least that he was aware of), he was welcome anywhere he could wish to go; the ladies of the houses often plying him with fresh baked cakes and the like, and the menfolk stopping to chat amicably.

The day being a fine one, Christopher stood up from the flower bed and stretched his back. He squinted up first at the clear sky and warming sun, then off into the distance. Enough time had been spent in the garden for one day, and his mother was visiting an elderly neighbour. He would not be missed if he should wander about. Strolling into the house, he took up his drawing papers, and pencils, and set out. He walked first to the road, then ambled along it by way of bordering meadows until he was nearly to Cherrybrook.

Looking off to the north, he noticed some grand old willows swaying in the wind, their shimmering fronds disappearing from view behind the verge. Where willows danced, there was usually water. With a smile, he carefully pushed his way through the swaying meadow grasses, and made his way towards the trees.

Perhaps he had willed to find her, and that is why he had walked nearly all the way to Cherrybrook, but he preferred to believe at that moment that it was providence. For, as he entered the canopy of willow branches, he saw Miss Hamblin, the lady who had so forcefully affected him at the dance. Here she was with a small paintbox (unless he was mistaken), sitting upon a log, and leaning forward with a brush to dab at a painting of... of what? He could not tell from such a distance. He would greet her politely and that would be all. She appeared to be alone, unchaperoned. He could not stay long under the circumstances.

As silently as possible, he crouched to set down his drawing kit next to a young oak tree that he would pass again on his way back home. He thought it best to hide his supplies, for if she saw him carrying his materials, he might not have the needed resolve to leave, if she should ask him to stay. She was altogether too interesting to him as it was.

Having set down his drawing tablet and pencils, Christopher purposely made a lot of noise, stepping forward and saying loudly enough for her to hear, yet hoping not to frighten her, "Miss Hamblin?"

She started, and turned quickly, her eyes wide.

"I shall not trespass long on your time alone," he said, removing his hat and bowing, "but I happened out for a walk and saw these magnificent willows from the road and thought I would see what natural beauty it held inside." He silently acknowledged that he had found an altogether different beauty than expected.

Miss Hamblin reminded him of a swan. She had a light complexion with dark eyes and rich, dark hair which, like all proper ladies, she kept pinned up. She had an elegant neck and a graceful way of moving, even the turn of her head made her seem like a living work of art. There was something else, a strength held in check, that did nothing to upset the swanlike impression.

At first, she appeared frightened. It was unavoidable as a young lady alone out of doors. But when she realised who he was, she smiled so warmly at him that he dared to take a few steps forward.

"Why, Mr. Morton, aren't you curious about what I am painting?" she called. "Come closer and you may see."

Christopher took another quick look around in case there was someone nearby to carry a tale of secret rendezvous back to Wellsey or Cherrybrook. Seeing no one, he moved through the waving grass toward her. He would look at her artwork, he told himself, and then bid her good day.

When he drew closer, he saw that she had a small wooden board with a paper tacked to it, leaned against a gnarled root. She was painting the furthest edge of the pond where the willows waved over the water, and the clearing beyond the trees. The foreground had good depth, despite its unfinished state, and the distant field and sky in the centre of the picture were light and airy, with deftly painted clouds.

As if they were friends of longstanding, and not awkward new acquaintances, she bit the inside of her cheek and squinted up at him for a moment and then back at the scene before them.

"Well? What am I missing? Anything?" she asked.

All was quiet while Christopher considered an opinion.

At that precise moment, a flock of birds that had gathered in one of the willows burst from the shadows of the trees, with a great deal of screeching and wing flapping, and flew away.

"Birds," suggested Christopher seriously, and they both laughed. "The timing was perfect. I could not resist! No, I do not think your picture is lacking a thing." He smiled as his eyes scanned the painting. "Indeed, it is very lovely, I think you have a strong composition to begin with and everything follows well from that."

"And?" she prompted, in a teasing tone.

"Are you asking me to praise you more?" Christopher chuckled, his eyes sparkling.

"No, I shall have my parents do that," she laughed. "Obviously you have an eye for art if you tell me that I have 'a strong composition'. Tell me more, will you not?"

Christopher glanced down into her earnest, laughing eyes, and then looked up again quickly. It was best to stay focused on the landscape rather than the nearer scenery, however beautiful.

He tilted his head judiciously, eying the painting. "All right," he said consideringly, "I like the delicacy that it has. It has movement, which is necessary for a convincing sketch out-of-doors. The colours, being in watercolour, are soft, yet there is proper contrast between light and shadow. Does that suit you, Miss Hamblin?"

"Bravo!" She said, setting her brush down and turning to face him. "Surely, you must be a painter yourself?" She looked down shyly, "I confess that I know you draw, for I have seen your drawings."

Christopher nodded in comprehension. "When you came for impromptu tea that morning." He went on, "No, I do not paint, but I appreciate art of all manners. I never can see too much of it. I confess, it fascinates me!"

Miss Hamblin wrinkled her nose and held a hand over her eyes to shade them. "It is a daily pleasure for you then, to have the Deposition in your vestry."

"Yes," he answered plainly. He had the feeling that Cherise wanted to know more about it than he could disclose, but he was not at liberty to say more. "I draw because I cannot seem to manage colour! It is enough for me to capture contrast and contours, I'm afraid."

"I understand." Miss Hamblin nodded sympathetically. "I suppose that is why I am often discontent with my work. The colours captivate me and then I lose my edges."

He chuckled and smiled at her again. "I think watercolour must suit you then, Miss Hamblin, for that is the chief charm of the medium. Is it not considered so?"

"It is. But perhaps someday I shall try my hand at more serious painting."

"And I should face my fears of colours, and challenge myself to try painting, of any sort."

A roguish expression came over Miss Hamblin's face, and she said, "You must be one of those persons that finds contours comforting. I comprehend it, but cannot quite manage to stay in the lines."

Christopher looked at her in bemusement. "Are we still speaking of art? ...or have we moved on to practical philosophy?"

Miss Hamblin laughed. "I do not intend my art to reflect my personality, and while there are similarities, I take a far more relaxed view of my painting techniques than my personal choices. And you?" She squinted at him, "How is life as a vicar?" She bent her head and swished her brush in the small water jar. "Is it all shadows, lights, and staying in the lines?" She glanced up at him and then turned back to her painting and he could not see her face. She loaded a thin brush and deftly flicked in lines to imitate branches. She asked, "Are you a vicar by your own choice, or someone else's?"

He was conscious that he could keep her at a distance by giving a polite answer, but on impulse he decided to speak from his heart. "I knew the church suited me from when I was but a boy of ten," he confided. "I had grown up without a father, you see, so I trotted about after our very patient church curate, carrying things for him, generally making myself useful in my childish way. That same curate, the first one, was my tutor for a few years, as well. He gave me a very good start to my education." He paused for a moment and gazed up at the sky. "My mother is a clever woman and, as a woman left with a young son to raise alone, she managed as best she could to rear me in country gentility. Neither of us have ever known want, fortunately. In fact, if there was something that that good woman felt I needed for the improvement of my mind or betterment of my soul, we always had enough funds for it."

And in this fashion, they continued on, lost in open and friendly discourse, as if they had been childhood friends or brother and sister. Almost.

Christopher couldn't remember ever having spoken so freely to a young lady before, or having met one as curious about the same artistic and intellectual ideas that frequently occupied his own mind. The time passed very agreeably. He glanced up at the sun, and with a shock, realised that he ought to have left long ago.

Miss Hamblin must have seen the change in his face, for she grew quiet and she bit the inside of her cheek again.

It was not his place to comfort her, however. It could only lead to thoughts that, as a nameless vicar, he had no right to think of in connection with a lady of her quality. Even though their towns were small, old titles and entails weighed heavily.

He stood suddenly, for he had unconsciously sunk to the ground at her feet, sitting in the grass, talking, listening, ...watching her.

"It has been a pleasure, Miss Hamblin. A pleasure that I shall long remember, but ought not repeat." His brow knit as he looked intently into her eyes, scanning every detail of her face as if hoping to commit this moment to memory.

She looked back at him, unblinking. A soft, rosy blush made her look all the more beautiful, but still she did not demure. Then, finally, she blinked and looked down. Slowly, she reached for her bonnet and tied it under her chin. He watched her pretty hands and fingers, longing to touch them. After she had finished tying her ribbons, she faced him and said very gravely, "I understand and agree completely. I shall not mention that we met today, for there is nothing that transpired that I need confess, nor you. We met by ... fortunate accident, Mr. Morton. Good day."

"My name is Christopher. In case you wish to know. Please, what is your given name, Miss Hamblin?"

"Cherise," she answered.

Christopher bowed politely, then with a great deal of willpower, smiled sorrowfully, as if he were already smiling at a memory instead of a living, breathing friend. Turning reluctantly away, he walked back the way he had come, stooping to pick up his drawing kit as he passed the oak tree.

Chapter Five

In the weeks that followed, Cherise went several times more to paint by the willows. She knew she went in large part hoping Mr. Morton would be there and, if she happened to hear any movement from the direction of Wellsey, she looked around in expectation, only to discover that the sound had been made by a squirrel, bird, or the movement of the wind.

The vicar never did repeat his visit to Carter's Pond when she was there, but she suspected that he came sometimes when she did not, for there was a new, barely visible path worn in the grass from the direction of Wellsey.

Her own eager expectation to see and converse with the vicar necessarily concerned her. Cherise was forced to remind herself many times over that she could not entertain a courtship from the vicar, no matter how powerful an attraction she felt. Despite the wretched conclusion that Mr. Morton could never be a suitor, she refused to toss away the intense desire she had for his friendship.

After breakfast one morning, she removed herself to her room and sat at her desk. After drifting in quiet thought for a little while, she took up her pen and drew a flock of blackbirds scattering at the top of the stationery paper and beneath them she wrote:

"Friend,

This is such a fine place to draw or paint, please make use of it. I never come on Mondays, Sundays or Thursdays, so you may enjoy it in solitude. Other than the birds. You must share the view with the birds.

Yours respectfully, etc."

And she left the signature blank.

Snatching up her satchel and tiny painter's box, she hurried off to Carter's Pond.

That day, after she had finished a painting sketch that she wrathfully declared a "rotter" and "bound for a roaring blaze at home," she tucked her letter to the vicar inside a hole in the log where she often sat. She found a place to wedge it, where she hoped it would be safe from rain but discoverable by anyone who sat just where she did.

When she had completed this whimsical task, she felt faintly cheerful. If it worked, and Mr. Morton should find her note and leave one for her, it would provide a thread of communication between them that seemed otherwise impossible. On the contrary, if she came back to find the letter undisturbed, she knew she would feel disappointed, but until that day should arrive, she had hope. She hastened home with a lighter heart than she'd had in days.

The first couple of times that Cherise returned to the pond she found only her own letter, but on her third visit, it had been replaced with a very small, tightly folded paper written in a very precise hand. Her pulse quickened as she read it.

"Friend,

I was pleased to discover your note. I have been occupied of late with news of an artistic nature. I cannot share specifics, but you shall soon hear of what is on its way to our corner of the country! I cannot wait to bask in the hope and inspiration that I fully expect it shall provide.

If you could cross the ocean only once in your life and were guaranteed a safe passage and return home, where would you go, and why?

That question should keep you busy for a while. Or, perhaps not. You are rather likely to be the type of person to have already given serious thought to audacious longings for world exploration.

I will tell you mine at once. I would go to Venice. That city captures my heart like none other. It is a place of colour and architecture, and of course, art.

Yours respectfully etc."

After having read the little letter over and over in the privacy of the trees, Cherise felt as though she floated home. She crossed through the house quickly, hoping to be unnoticed, but stumbled on the stairs in her eagerness to draft a reply.

Her mother was passing through the central hall and must have heard Cherise's misstep, for she took a step backward in order to make eye contact and called out, "Whatever is the matter, dear? Were you chased home by a pack of hunting dogs?"

Cherise held the banister railing and tried to manufacture a reason for her clumsiness, but all she could come up with was, "I think I am overheated. It is a very warm day." She did not stop long enough to observe her mother's reaction.

Cherise and Christopher kept up a lively correspondence throughout the first weeks of summer. Mindful that someone else might intercept their letters, the subject matter was sometimes intellectual, sometimes humorous, but always respectful of the social gulf between them.

They saw each other in person very seldom. If their paths did accidentally cross, it was in public, and they acted as though they were mere acquaintances. It was wretched to have to be content with a quick look, a polite greeting, and be done at that, but after having been discovered by her mother at the dance, Cherise did her best not to raise suspicions about her feelings for Mr. Morton. She tried to convince herself it was for the best that they could not meet in person, for it could only make their interminable separation more painful, but she ached for the excitement of it. She trusted herself to keep secrets, but could she trust Christopher to do the same? His clear eyes might easily betray his thoughts. In the end she was forced to conclude that, although she longed to speak with him face to face, it was better that she did not.

Therefore, when Lady Hamblin told her daughter that the Mortons' name appeared on the same guest list as theirs did for a dinner party at Penfield House, Cherise was both thrilled and terrified. She retreated to the garden to better think it over in the privacy of the hedges. If anyone had been watching her, they would have seen her pacing the herb bed as though she were a sheepdog on duty, her imagination hard at work.

Finally, the date inscribed on the Penfield dinner party invitation arrived, and Cherise waited for the finishing touches on her hair late that afternoon. The only external sign of nervousness was a slight jiggling of her foot, which her maid quickly put an end to by drawing attention to it.

What she was still considering at this late hour, was how she was to comfortably manage being in the same room with Lord Penfield and the appealing Mr. Morton. It was going to require a great deal of diplomacy. She mustn't throw herself toward Mr. Morton, despite her temptation to do so. She had already spent many miserable hours contemplating the many ways they would suit, and all the ways that her parents and society would object. Nor could she ruin her prospects with the Viscount under the watchful eyes of her parents. The Kent sisters would be guests as well. Was the Viscount playing matchmaker? The Mortons and the Kents were close to being on equal footing in terms of social status. Even though it was unfair of her, the thought of Mr. Morton courting one of the Kents made her insides roil with bitterness.

And soon, she may have to leave Cherrybrook and Mr. Morton for the remainder of the summer. For the past two and a half months, Cherise had been enduring her parents' (most especially her mother's) hints about the London Season.

"Your father and I know this is *your* year," her mother had quipped. "It is your turn now. Last summer was such a crush, you know."

She knew. Cherise recalled last summer with clarity; the way she had been carted around from dressmaker to milliner, and made to stand stone-still, holding her breath, while lean, muscular women tugged at her stays and forced her to take small, "delicate" breaths in practice for the dance rooms. And even that literal squeeze was not the crush her mother spoke of. That had been the excess of young women like herself, a little below the best of the ton; those who had fought to get there or had been dragged in by a parent or sponsor in hopes of being noticed by one of the handful of gentlemen of "suitable heritage", all other assets of age, personality, or even morality, aside.

The only aspects of town life that Cherise looked forward to were the cultural entertainments. She was fascinated by the variety of people and how they dressed. She could stay all day in a museum or a gallery and never once complain of boredom. And last year, she had been allowed to take her painting set with her, so that when she was not at a dance or party (or getting dressed for one), she had been allowed to paint. There were inspiring musicals and lectures upon occasion, too. Sadly, her father was far more likely to allow her to attend them than her mother. Lady Hamblin thought such lofty ideas and even art galleries made Cherise "too blue."

And thus, what was to be done about Lord Penfield now? Cherise disliked him and always had, but as the pressure to marry increased, the best *local* match began to appear at an advantage over any of the men she had met last year. For if she accepted Lord Penfield, she would hardly be leaving home. Penfield was so near. She could visit her parents as often as she wished, as well as paint in all of her favourite places. The Viscount was seldom home and, as far as conversation went, he scarcely would notice if she said nothing at all! Her presence would merely provide him the audience he seemed to crave. This far she could consider. The unfathomable difficulty was in contemplating *ever* doing him that service which would provide him his "heir and a spare". Beyond that, he would find his own amorous amusements. It was common enough. Still, she wondered at her parents. Why did they push her under his nose? She supposed it to be because Lord Penfield's father had been so much *more* in the height of his influence.

The Earl was haughty and private, but he had good taste and knew when to hold his tongue, unlike his son. And now there was a new problem in the person of Mr. Morton. Could she bear to live as the lonely, lady patroness of Cherrybrook and watch him marry someone else, or perhaps the more torturous, see him remain unwed, a constant reminder of what could not be?

As these thoughts did nothing to stop her foot from tapping, she took control of herself and forcibly put them from her mind. The only way to handle the evening was to treat Mr. Morton as a friendly acquaintance for the safety of her own and his reputation, and to treat Lord Penfield as a calculated potential alliance. *It would be easily done*, she lied to herself, *nothing at all to worry about*.

"I am finished, miss. You look lovely."

"Am I ready for battle?" Cherise asked with a dry laugh as she surveyed her coiffured hair.

"Lord Penfield may be struck down speechless," responded her maid. "Aye, you're that elegant."

Cherise's eyes met Susan's briefly in the mirror. "Thank you, Susan. You have bolstered my confidence. I hope you have a relaxing evening with nothing that needs attending but a good meal."

"Thank you, miss," curtseyed Susan as she left her mistress.

Cherise stood tall and, with as deep of a breath as she could muster in tight stays and a fashionable gown, she put her chin up and smiled at her reflection before sweeping from the room and down the stairs to meet her parents.

"You look very fine this evening, Miss Hamblin," declared the Viscount with a bow as he greeted her, eyeing her up and down.

"Thank you, Lord Penfield," Cherise responded civilly. She smiled politely at their host, and reminded herself not to flinch tonight if he continued to look at her the way he was doing now; like a fox at a partridge. Goodness, he didn't even like her. Not really. It must be the dress.

"Is his lordship joining us this evening?" asked her father, hopefully.

"I regret to say he is not," admitted Lord Penfield, dragging his hungry gaze away from Cherise. "He no longer is able to join me at the table even on good days, unfortunately. He sends his regards."

With his attention shifted to her mother and father, Cherise quickly looked around at the small party. Likely she and her parents were the last to arrive, for there were the Kents, the Terrences, three unattached gentlemen, Lord Nye, Mr. Davies, and Mr. Fox, whom Cherise recognized as town friends of the Viscount's. And finally, the Mortons.

She intentionally made eye contact across the hall with Mrs. Morton before slowly transferring her gaze to the lady's magnetic son. He was standing next to his mother near the doorway to the best parlour, conversing with Lord Nye and Miss Teresa Kent.

"Mrs. Morton," said Cherise, again focusing on the older woman and swishing forward with her gloved hand outstretched. Once she was near, she looked up at Christopher. She struggled to breathe naturally whilst meeting his eyes, "-and Mr. Morton! How lovely to see you both again."

Mr. Morton opened his blue eyes wide, and said innocently, "Miss Hamblin? How happy we are to see you again. Delighted." Christopher kept his hands behind his back and bowed slightly. Then he looked about the room in the way one does when making conversation with a stranger.

Mrs. Morton stood very near, and appeared to be watching her son carefully. Cherise wondered how much she knew of Christopher's walks. She could not tell if his mother was curious or anxious, only that her usual easy smile seemed taut, and her lips were pressed together, as were her gloved hands. She seemed older tonight than previously. And somehow... frail, a word Cherise had never before thought of in connection to the vicar's mother.

Mr. Morton's gaze fixed momentarily upon a portrait in an unoccupied corner of the hall, then he looked again at Cherise and said, "You must know that Lord Stafford has an impressive collection of artworks. Perhaps, if you are not weary of the collection, our host will give us a tour this evening?"

"I think that is a splendid idea, Mr. Morton! You do not often enjoy the gallery here?"

"It is true that I am a regular caller, but because the Earl is far from well, I am here in my professional capacity, and I visit him in his rooms. He likes me to read through my sermons aloud, but he seldom speaks." He paused. "Any effort beyond a single word or sentence carries him into a spasm of coughing." A shadow crossed Mr. Morton's face, but then he seemed to return to happier thoughts. "When I arrived to be introduced to Lord Stafford last October, he had made his study in the corner of the gallery, and I confess I was overwhelmingly pleased with what I saw! It would have been impolite to linger too long that day, so I welcome-" He would have continued, but his mother took him by the arm and, by her expression, the swift movement seemed to be a warning. Cherise darted a look toward her own parents, who were moving purposefully in her direction.

Lady Hamblin had lifted her chin, striking a regal pose, and Cherise saw a slight crease between her mother's eyes, then a sudden chilly smile followed by a pointed look at Lord Penfield's back. Cherise knew that she was receiving her first censure of the evening.

Christopher and his mother should not be expected to bear up with the artificial friendliness of Lord Penfield or, indeed, her parents. Before Mr. Morton should attempt anything chivalrous, Cherise stepped forward and said rather archly, "Penfield, we were just saying how good of you it would be to give us a tour of your art collection. I know it to be... extensive," she was pleased with herself for having gotten a sort of breathy tone into her voice on that last word.

Lord Penfield puffed out his chest, and with a toothy grin, reached out for Cherise and set her hand on his arm. "Just so, madam," he smirked. Then addressing himself to the others he announced that they were all invited for a stroll through the gallery with Miss Hamblin and himself.

Cherise felt somewhat triumphant. She had gotten her way, *their* way, by entreating Lord Penfield to give her and the Mortons something interesting to see and talk about before her parents should have an opportunity to intimidate them. However, when she looked to Mr. Morton for affirmation, she saw his jaw was firmly set, and he did not meet her eyes.

She watched as he led his mother to the rear of the hall to a life-size standing portrait of the Earl. They did not seem to care a straw for what the others thought of them as they conducted their own little portrait gallery tour. They appeared to be in a world of their own.

Cherise felt strangely confused and more than a trifle unsettled. Her breath caught in her throat, but she dragged her attention away from the Mortons and forced herself to focus instead on Penfield's exposition on the family portraits that hung in the portion of the entry hall nearest the front door.

There were several small pieces to catch one's eye, but they were easily outshone by an enormous painting of the middle-aged Earl. In this piece, Lord Stafford had his head held high and one hand confidently holding his jacket lapel, the other resting upon the shoulder of his wife, who was seated next to him on a silk-covered chair. The heir, Lord Penfield, stood nearly between them, his legs and arms crossed elegantly. This wasn't the first time Cherise had been to Penfield House, and she thought this time (just as she had thought the other times) that it was interesting, and somehow tragic, how the three people in the painting could be in such close proximity, yet look so detached from one other, so ill at ease in one another's company.

The Mortons had begun to cross the room to join the others and, just when Cherise would speak to them, the Viscount stepped in front of her, effectively blocking them from her view, and ushered the small party to the back wall where the canvas of the young Earl hung.

Cherise had always rather liked this one. The Earl looked nothing like this in real life that she could remember. His expression was so pleasant in this picture. It was not that he smiled exactly, but there was a sort of romantic, dreamy aspect to his eyes and mouth. Lord Penfield was saying, "... And this, of course, is my father when he was in the prime of his youth. I am not certain who commissioned the work, whether it was he himself or my grandfather. I should someday, I suppose, make the effort to look into the matter by asking him or checking our records. At any rate, a few of you present were acquainted with my father in those days, a handful of years before he married my mother."

Cherise's gaze strayed to the Mortons once more. They had not followed the group down the hall, but had by now stepped away from the large family portrait. Their heads were bent close together, and Mrs. Morton leant heavily upon her son's arm. Only when Lord Penfield announced that they should *all* proceed into the gallery did the distracted pair look up and slowly re-join the rest of the party. Lord Penfield cast a glance over his shoulder and he sniffed proudly, patting Cherise's hand as he led her on his arm with everyone following behind on their way down the wide hallway. After bidding her to enter the gallery ahead of him, Lord Penfield released her hand reluctantly and stood against the wall ushering each of the other guests forward after Cherise. Once the Mortons were inside, Penfield called out loudly, "Wilcox, see to it that drinks are brought to us! We will enjoy the gallery until it is time for dinner."

His man nodded his head and said, "yes, milord," and darted away.

It really was an impressive collection. After Penfield's feeble store of knowledge had been spent, Cherise struggled to hear what Mr. Morton was telling his mother about the particulars of various pieces, but it was best not to stand too near. Several times his warm gaze clutched at her, and that brief moment of eye contact was enough. It had to be.

At supper, Cherise found herself placed at the right hand of her host, who was leaned back, deep into his chair. He was drumming his fingers on its carved arms, listening to two simultaneous conversations and throwing out what Cherise thought to be contentious comments now and again in the direction of the Kents. He smirked at the result, and seemed more pleased than ever when Mr. Morton was forced to keep the peace in the midst of the Kents' petty squabbles.

At last, the exhausting evening came to a close. Cherise felt cheated of what had been one of her only opportunities to talk to the Mortons. For instead of earnest conversation with people she was interested in knowing better, she had been forced to give her attention to the Viscount and watch the Misses Kents bold attempts to monopolise the vicar.

Chapter Six

Some weeks after the dinner party at Penfield House, Christopher finished in the gardens as the sun was setting. Surveying his handiwork, he decided he was pleased with himself, but his aching shoulders attested to the long hours he had spent moving rocks, hauling compost and digging up plants. He hummed a sweet, but slightly melancholy melody about summer's end as he made his way to the back door of the vicarage.

He paused at the top step and brushed off his boots, squinting into the warm night air, savouring the deep blues, pinks and purples which made up the colour palette of twilight. He unlaced his boots and opened the back door. As he stepped stocking-footed into the hall near the kitchen, he heard his mother call out, "Christopher? You are coming in later and later each evening."

He entered the sitting room and once his eyes had adjusted to the cosy but dim interior, he saw that she sat doing needlework near a window in the last light of day. She glanced at him over the tops of her spectacles before returning to her stitching.

Smiling, he crossed the room to her. "Perhaps it is not that I am coming in later, Mother," he said, kissing her on the forehead, "but that the days are growing shorter."

"Nonsense! We have only just passed the height of summer," she replied coolly.

"And look at you," Christopher bent down and peered at her. "You are straining your eyes with your night sewing!" he said teasingly.

His mother looked up with a quick grin. "When you were a boy, I might have called you to task for contradicting me, but you are right, I suppose. Forgive me."

"There is nothing to forgive in what you say," said Christopher as he backed away and dropped wearily into an oak and leather chair. "Perhaps I do need to pay more attention to the hours and take more ease."

"Yes," agreed his mother, leaning forward and dropping her stitchery in her lap as though it had been stage property, merely for show. "You ought to hire a gardener to assist you. Not for any of the aspects of the garden work which delight you, for I know some of it surely does, but you could hire a man to help out with the fine work, keeping the beds, weeding, mulching and the like."

"I cannot imagine it proper for a vicar to hire yet another servant," Christopher re-joined quickly.

"I thought you must object, but I have already given it some thought. You might hire a fellow from town that needs the work but wouldn't live here, for I know that would not do. Nor do we have the room." She turned slightly in her chair, moved the draperies a little and looked out. The night was falling quickly, but one could still see the outline of the church against a backdrop of trees and a peach-coloured sky. "How is the new church window?" she asked, facing her son once more. "Have you received news of when it is ready to be installed?"

"Happily, yes! It is to be finished and ready to unveil by All Saint's Day." With his thumb, Christopher absent-mindedly massaged a callous on his hand. "I trust I do not need to remind you that it is an anonymous donation?"

"I have told no one, just as I promised. But since you are determined to spend such a tidy sum on art for the church, what is a very small amount to spend on pay for a gardener?"

Christopher watched his mother take up her sewing again. She seemed so sure that she would get her way and that he would soon be asking around town for an assistant. She began to hum softly. She had a mellifluous voice and it had always soothed him, but this time he felt as though she might be using it to avoid further discussion. He slid down in his chair, his long frame stretched out in front of it. With his feet crossed at the ankles and with his elbows on the chair arms, he put his fingertips together under his chin and studied her carefully before speaking again; this time upon a related subject which must be addressed (although he held little hope that she would answer him).

"I think now that this most recent financial increase must be from my father's estate? For it is beyond what your own family could spare, or would think advisable." He paused to see how she might respond.

She did not look up but rather repositioned her spectacles and looked down intently at the handwork in her lap. As he had expected, she would not answer. With a small sigh, Christopher relinquished the desire to press her about the matter. "The painting and window are ways that I can use my wealth for good. As a country vicar, to what better use can I put it?"

She looked at him curiously for a few moments before returning to her sewing. Christopher waited silently, listening to the gentle popping and pulling sounds of his mother's stitching as she punctured the material and pulled the thread through. Eventually, the grandfather clock chimed, and Mrs. Morton glanced up at her son before gently folding and setting aside her sewing. She pressed a thumb and forefinger into her temples and rubbed them slowly as if she had a headache. "I find I am quite tired. Even though it is early, I think I shall retire for the night." Rising slowly from her chair, and groaning a little, as though her knees were stiff, she asked again, "You will inquire about garden help then, won't you?"

Brows creased, Christopher nodded thoughtfully and said, "If it pleases you." Before his mother walked away, he added, "perhaps you are lonely. Is that it? You are left too much alone in the evening when it is most pleasant to have one another to talk to."

Mrs. Morton smiled wistfully. "I am not lonely, no. However, it would benefit you to remember that I will not last forever." She gazed down at him a little sadly. "I feel it sometimes. And when the time comes when I am no longer an easy companion, *you* may be lonely."

Christopher frowned. He couldn't remember his mother speaking to him before of her own mortality. She paused next to his chair, reached out her hand and patted his head very lightly, just as she had done when he was a small boy.

"Goodnight, Christopher," she said quietly as she moved past him.

"Goodnight, Mother."

He sat still for a moment, then turned to address her retreating form. "You would tell me if you were ailing or troubled in any way?"

She halted and said, "I would, yes."

He heard her slowly wind her way through the corridor and up the stairs as she prepared for bed. Putting his hands behind his head, he leaned back in his chair and thought about all she had said. Christopher decided that beginning tomorrow, he would make a special effort to come in earlier or ask his mother out for a short walk in the mornings before he went to the church.

The following week, Mrs. Morton received a letter from her sister inviting her to come and stay for as long as she could be spared. Christopher felt that such a holiday would be a welcome diversion and perhaps just the thing to revive his mother's flagging spirits.

"I am certain you should go," pronounced Christopher when she read him the letter at breakfast. "But do not extend your stay past what we have agreed upon or I shall be forced to talk to myself in the evenings. And, since I know all of my own stories, I would soon make tedious company, I assure you," he said with a chuckle.

A faint smile turned up a corner of Mrs. Morton's mouth and she said affectionately. "You ought to marry, Christopher." She lifted her chin as if challenging him to disagree, but her eyes were merry. She looked around the room and then leaned forward to whisper, "And I think I know who the young woman is."

Christopher was uncomfortable. Had he been careless at Penfield that evening? Had he revealed his partiality for Miss Hamblin? He was instantly annoyed with himself for allowing his mind to race to Cherise. He forced himself to respond to his mother in the same playful tone that she had taken with him. "Do you imply that I have not yet been introduced to the lady, or that I do not know that I ought to marry her?"

"Oh, do not tease me," replied his mother patiently. "Only, I will say this: it would please me for you to remember that social disparities are not as insurmountable as you might believe them to be." Christopher looked at her, perplexed, but she would speak no more on that head. Instead, she began listing tasks that he would need to undertake while she was away. "One thing that you must do is to take the charity baskets around. I shall make a list for you of the regulars."

"Excellent. Thank you, Mother," said Christopher as he wiped his mouth and finished his tea. He was eager to avoid further comment upon his matrimonial condition. "Make me a list and I will look it over to be sure I understand what is expected of me. Will that be all?"

"You will give Thea the menus each Monday. I will prepare them for you. If I think of anything else, I will put it to paper." She eyed him judiciously. "You go on now. I see you are ready to be off to the church."

He grinned and rose from the table, but before leaving his mother to get on with the pleasant task of accepting her sister's invitation, he said, "I hope that you will have a wonderful stay with Aunt Griffiths, and come back well rested and restored. I can see that moving to Wellsey has been a difficult adjustment, and I hope that a visit with your sister will be just the thing to ease your mind."

"Is the basket ready?" Christopher called from the front hall as he adjusted the lapels of his jacket before heading out on visitations.

Theodora, their head kitchen maid, came rushing in with a cumbersome basket with eggs from their chickens, several loaves of bread, butter, and jellies. Christopher took the basket from her with thanks, and set off over the footbridge and out toward the road by way of the church.

Before leaving the previous day for his aunt's, his mother had told him which three households to visit first, before he was to fetch a second basket from Penfield House for another three houses. It would make for a full morning.

The first house he called upon was in a merry state for, while they had little enough by way of possessions (and their house was badly in need of repair), they were rich in affection and good health, and had just welcomed a new baby into their midst.

The next two houses were inhabited by elderly members of the village, frail, and in need of conversation as much as full bellies. This suited Christopher, for he loved how much his neighbours lit up when he took interest in their lives. One of his favourite things to do was to ask a parishioner (especially an elderly one), to tell him their best story. Listening as they sorted their way through their ideas aloud (for they scarcely could resist muttering and chuckling over stories) never ceased to delight him as much as it cheered them to reminisce. *I will have to ask Miss Hamblin for her favourite story. I have not yet asked her.* The thought came unbidden as thoughts of Cherise often did. His heart soared for a moment as he imagined listening to her velvet laughter and watching her lively brown eyes and pretty mouth as she talked. But then it plummeted again when he remembered whose child she was. He took a deep breath. Well, perhaps she could write a story out for him. He would ask her in a letter. It would be better to read her favourite story than never to learn it.

After seeing to the needs of the family in the third cottage, Christopher strode off for Penfield House. On this occasion, he was not here to sit with his benefactor. There were more baskets to be delivered. As he turned into the yard, his attention was arrested by a small commotion near the front door.

Lord Penfield came bursting into view. He was dressed in travelling attire, followed by a pack of nervous servants led by Mr. Poole, Penfield's long-suffering butler. Behind Mr. Poole was Lord Penfield's valet, carrying a valise in each hand, and James and Harry, the red-haired footmen, each shouldering a large travelling trunk. Christopher stood politely aside, and watched as the Viscount climbed into the waiting coach, firing out clipped commands.

"I shall be back shortly," Penfield barked at Poole from the open carriage door. "I will return at the start of the hunting season if I am not summoned to my father's side before then. Send word of his condition. I am off now!" And he slammed the door. Once his trunks were stowed, the driver moved the carriage quickly out of the yard and into the lane.

When Lord Penfield had gone, Christopher slipped around the back of the main house and knocked at the service door.

A kitchen maid answered, curtseyed quickly, and pulled the empty basket from his hand, offering him a chair just inside the door as she hurried off. When she returned, she showed him that the basket contained several jars of soup, loaves of freshly-baked brown bread, as well as a large cheese.

"What's in the basket goes to the sick families, the Smiths, Lapthams and Clarks. But this bag," she said looking down and jabbing at a largish bag on the floor with a worn toe of her boot, "goes to Mr. Keevey. Keevey is the farmer who fell off his roof last week. Poor man is down on his luck again." She made a clicking noise with her tongue. "Aye. That's the way of it sometimes. His wife passed on last summer and he's got two young ones left on 'is hands."

"Has he never attended church? I do not recall ever having met a Mr. Keevey," said the vicar, wonderingly.

"Begging your pardon, sir, if he has not. Mr. Keevey's likely not made it to a service, what with all that's happened to him and all, and him living so far. Here," she said, tucking a scrap of paper in the basket, "I had Cook write out directions to his house. It's a fine way out, it is, so you'll want to ride there. Keevey is Cook's cousin, you see. Good it's you this week and not your poor mum! On account of the babies, and him being laid up, we thought he might be needing a little extra. Tell him it's courtesy of Tilly, that's 'is cousin, and Penfield 'ouse. Thank you kindly, sir."

Christopher nodded, thanked the girl warmly, and headed around to the front of the house and on into town.

Again, he spent time listening with patience and compassion to the complaints of the members of the houses that he ministered to. The Smiths were a perilously thin, spider-like elderly couple who had no children to look after them, but Christopher was relieved to see that, today anyway, there was a bright young woman lending a hand and doing some tidying. Aside from a shy glance upon entry, she scarcely looked around while he was there talking to Mr. and Mrs. Smith, but he recognized her as a member of his parish. Her name was Miss

Prentice, and she came on Sundays and holy days as the head of her household in a manner that rather reminded him of a mother goose, with two younger sisters, and three small brothers in tow behind her. They sat in the back, nearly always the last to arrive and the first to leave. Each wore clothes that were shabbily genteel, nearly outgrown, some patched, but always clean and pressed for church. He thought at first that they must live alone, but he was informed that, although their mother had recently died, their father lived but did not attend services.

By the time he took his leave, Miss Prentice was nowhere to be seen.

The second home was that of a widow sick with fever. Her daughter was with her and reported to Christopher in hushed tones that her mother had turned the corner on the malady, thank the Lord, and seemed to be improving by the hour.

Next were the Clarks. He had to stoop under the beams to enter the Clarks' kitchen, and had just set the basket on the table in order to unpack their portions, when he was surprised to see a familiar face. Miss Prentice came in carrying an arm full of wood. She stopped in the low doorway and coloured pink when she saw him standing there.

He smiled and nodded to her and said, "You were at Mr. and Mrs. Smiths' home not an hour ago. You are Miss Prentice are you not? Or perhaps a ministering angel or apparition?" he teased, as he crossed the room to relieve her of the wood.

"Aye," she replied, still blushing. "I am. I come every day to help the Clarks get their wood and I stop to make sure the Smiths have got enough to eat. They were friends of my mum's." Miss Prentice looked up at him shyly and gave a small laugh as she offered him the last small log she held, and wiped her hands on her apron. "I often see Mrs.

Morton here. She is one of the kindest women I have ever met. You are fortunate to have a mother like her." Miss Prentice looked down at the floor and then up at Christopher again. " I suppose she's gone off now to see her sister? She told us she was going away for a visit."

He bowed forward slightly in acknowledgement. "She has indeed. I'm afraid I am a clumsy substitute for her, but I see with you around, I need not fear that everything that *should* be done, *will* be done." Looking about the room with a smile, Christopher discovered the wood box near the cooking stove, and crossed the room to fill it. He spoke over his shoulder, "This is very good of you, Miss Prentice. Bless you," he said, standing up as best he could without striking his head on the low ceiling, "If you should need more food or supplies, you have only to ask, and I will do what I can to come to your aid."

Miss Prentice looked at the floor as she replied, "'Tis all right, Mr. Morton." Blushing again, she bobbed a curtsey and turned away, rolling up the sleeves of her dress as she headed for the pantry.

Impressed by her modesty and kindness, Christopher nodded approvingly and turned to the Clarks. Mr. Clark sat in a tattered, soft chair in the corner of the central room, coughing and wheezing, while Mrs. Clark scurried about, pulling out a pot and asking the Prentice girl to pour in the soup, and slice some cheese and bread. Seeing that they were quite well enough without him towering in their tiny home, Christopher picked up his hat and crossed the room to pray for Mr. Clark, before bidding the Clarks and Miss Prentice all good health and a good day.

Finding Mr. Keevey was his next commission, and it took him a rather long time. He discovered that the directions he had been given required keen observation- which he had aplenty- but also a knowledge of landmarks and local history that he did not yet possess. When he read the words "... take the left fork just past the broken fence at the north field after Perfoy farm," he stroked his chin. He might not know which farm belonged to the Perfoy family, but spotting broken fences and forks in the road sounded promising. Sure enough, after a short time he found what he was looking for and having taken the left fork and directed, he arrived at the Keevey cottage.

It was a small but tidy stone house. Everything was freshly painted and in working order. No broken fences here. The roof, although the old thatch style, was in good repair. But of course, it would be. Keevey had fallen from it, the kitchen girl at Penfield had said. In the dooryard there was a profusion of herbs and perennials with a healthy batch of thistles to boot. Christopher tied his horse to the front post and after reaching in to take up the awkward bag, strode up to the door and first knocked gently, then more forcefully.

He leaned forward, his ear to the door, to listen for activity within. Hearing nothing, he was just about to look for someplace to stow the bag where it would be safe from dogs or other curious animals, when he heard voices coming from around the back of the house, one certainly a man's and the second, a piping little voice of a young child.

Christopher backed away from the door and walked casually toward the gig, so that he would be in clear view of the Keeveys. The swishing grass and footsteps got louder and then a small child dashed out from the tall greenery and stopped abruptly upon seeing a stranger. The little one put her finger in her mouth bashfully and then turned back to look for her papa, who came moving more laboriously along the path.

"Hello, sir!" said the man in some surprise.

"Mr. Keevey is it?"

"You have that right. Who might you be? " The man smiled, his eyes crinkling pleasantly at the corners. A vicar, by the looks of you."

Mr. Keevey was deeply tanned with kind, dark eyes; eyes that held pain as well as gentleness. With one strong arm he held a baby, too young to walk, a bonneted little one in an abundance of overly large dresses. His other hand was protectively positioned over his ribs, likely to keep the infant from kicking or bumping his bruises.

"I come with kitchen gifts, I am to tell you, from Penfield House and most especially Tilly. She is your cousin?" Mr. Keevey smiled and nodded. "And you are correct, I am the new vicar at Wellsey, Mr. Morton at your service," Christopher beamed at the fellow; he couldn't help it, for there was something open about the man's manner that he instantly appreciated.

"Welcome, Mr. Morton. You see I have my hands full," The father had dropped his free hand down to the shy walking child who now grabbed his fingers tightly. The child continued to study Christopher with concern. Mr. Keevey glanced down and said quietly, "It's all right, Martha. This is Mr. Morton, and he has brought you something from Miss Tilly. Shall we invite him in and see what it is?"

Christopher followed as the man walked slowly and carefully up the few stone steps with the older child, Martha, in tow and the other in arms, peering over his shoulder with big, round eyes.

"Come in and take your ease, Mr. Morton. I can pour you a bit of ale for your troubles."

"We have never met before. Is that true?" asked Christopher as he pulled out a kitchen chair and sat down.

"That's right enough. I haven't had that pleasure. Tilly or her husband Jeffers often come here. We used to be in church regularly, but now..." his narrative trailed off as he walked to a corner of the kitchen and bent down, pulling a large, reed basket toward himself and setting the baby in it. The other child walked around the table to the side farthest from Christopher, and climbed up, sitting on her knees, watchfully. Keevey glanced awkwardly at the corner of the room where there was a lady's chair with a fine, needlepoint rose cover. Again, he rubbed his ribcage. "My wife passed on, you see. Last summer. She never recovered from the birth of little Lucy."

Christopher felt the heaviness of the man's spirits as the father looked down at his youngest daughter, and neither man spoke for several moments. "I am most truly sorry," said Christopher. Once Mr. Keevey raised his head again and had seemingly recovered, Christopher said with a gently encouraging smile, "Well, let me have some of this ale you mentioned, and I will gladly do any tasks that need doing. You took a fall, is that it?"

"Yes, a week ago. And it was right bad at first, I could hardly get myself out of bed, but I needed to, you understand," here, again, his gaze landed fondly on his children. "Still, I managed. They are good little girls and about as easy and quiet as a father could wish." Keevey smiled again and with a playful rap on the table, that made little Martha giggle, turned and pulled out two cups and a jug of ale and poured out two draughts, handing one to Christopher.

"Let me think," said Christopher. "What is it that a man cannot do for himself when he has gone and tumbled off a roof and has two babies to take care of? I suppose wood for the stove might need splitting and carrying."

"That would be helpful, sir. If I had known I was going to tumble, I would have prepared better," he said with a good-natured but shallow chuckle. It was obvious that it pained him to laugh.

Christopher smiled broadly. "From the looks of it, you run a tight ship. No escaped sheep or cows? No fences down?"

Mr. Keevey shook his head no. "Not that I know of. If you like to walk, next time you might take a ramble about and see if you notice anything out of place, but I think everything is in good order."

Christopher stood, leaving a goodly part of his ale unfinished, and touching the rim of the mug, said, "I believe I ought to earn the rest of this drink with some wood-splitting." He looked at the nearly empty firebox, "I'll bring in a few armloads and stack the rest where you like outside."

"Thank you again, Mr. Morton. While you do that, I will see what Tilly sent along." Martha was already poking at the bag with her dimpled fingers from where she sat at the table. Her father smiled as he drew the bag toward himself. "Aye, I imagine there is something sweet in there for you."

Christopher did not mind the occasional physical exertion of a labourer. He was not so much the gentleman that he would pass up an opportunity to work up a sweat. He had always liked sporting games at school, and was good at them.

He took off his jacket and collar, and stretched his shoulders, warming them before taking up the axe that was leaned nearby, and went to work. When he had finished and the wood was neatly stacked in piles, he took in a few armloads to put in the wood box, and set another small stack just outside the kitchen door.

Before leaving, he enjoyed the remainder of his ale. It was all the better-tasting after splitting wood, he told Keevey.

"If you'd like, I will plan to come at the same time on Thursday for more of the same good work, and same good ale, if you have it," he chuckled. "Are you certain there is nothing else that needs doing?"

Keevey shook his head, but Christopher sensed that he was thinking of something he did not want to say.

"You might as well say it," encouraged Christopher. "I can see that something has made you thoughtful."

Keevey picked up the baby, who had turned fussy, and began bouncing her gently in his arms. "I might say that, if you know of a woman to help with the washing and cooking, and who liked to hold a baby or two, I would be much obliged."

"A wife, you mean?" Christopher's eyebrows shot up.

Keevey looked at him quickly, "I doubt I will be that lucky, sir. You see there aren't kind-hearted women lining up to come out here, but I would be grateful for anyone to help for just a little while. I can pay and be respectful."

Christopher nodded sympathetically. "I will give your request some thought. Before too much time passes, I shall hope to have an introduction for you."

Christopher drove home thoughtfully. Not for the first time, he wondered at how Death was no respecter of persons. That fearsome Spector would steal away a much-needed mother of infants and a beloved wife from a man like Keevey, while selfish, even cruel, people sometimes lived long lives with robust health. Well, at least a man of Keevey's class was more likely to marry for love than, say, himself. In this regard, Christopher found he was envious. His mysterious paternity held him below the Hamblins, while his wealth put him above most families of Wellsey and Cherrybrook, making him a target for ambitious daughters, and sometimes their flirtatious mothers.

When he reached the vicarage, Christopher took up his drawing kit and headed back out into the open air. He hadn't intended to at the outset, but he walked all the way to The Artist's Folly, as he'd privately taken to calling the willow pond which he and Cherise shared together, yet separately. He'd scarcely had time enough to visit recently, and the busy fullness of the days ahead promised few, if any, walks in the direction of Cherrybrook. Knowing he had no right to care for her as much as he did, the dull pain of missing Miss Hamblin felt undeniably deserved.

All his worries vanished when he reached the fallen tree and found a letter waiting in her familiar hand. She wished to know how Lord Stafford was faring. Mrs. Terrance had given an unfavourable report to her mother, Lady Hamblin, and Cherise wanted to know if it was indeed true that the Earl was rapidly failing. With a sigh, Christopher sat on the log and whittled a point on his pencil and wrote back his report. At the conclusion, he remembered to ask Cherise for her best story. She could take her time with it, (he wrote), but he expected her to dwell on something pleasant for a while. He hoped her best story was a happy one. When he was finished, he folded the paper tightly and tucked it snuggly in the end of the cracked log.

Christopher headed for the church early the following morning. He wanted time alone, before the concerns of the day presented themselves. Starting his walk slowly, he savoured the flowery, balsamic scent of the lavender where some large bushes covered the footpath, their flower stalks bent low by the early morning rain. He hoped that his mother was discovering the same kind of morning. Probably she and Aunt Griffiths were enjoying their first cup of tea right at this very moment! The thought of them together brought a smile to his face.

This month would challenge him. He would be delivering the charity baskets on top of his studying, sermons, and other offices. He could afford to hire help for Keevey, although there was a level of pride in the man which made Christopher think that his offer might be refused. Keevey had understood his promise to come two or three times a week was not merely to help, but was an offering of friendship, of sincerest sympathy, and so it had been. Only now, the impracticalities of his impetuous offer were jostling for attention.

The footbridge to the church creaked as he strode across. A light, drizzling rain had begun and Christopher jammed his hands deep into his pockets to keep them dry. Just as he turned to the right and started down the narrow road that served as a drive to the churchyard, it began to rain in earnest, so he sped up his walk and nearly ran the last several yards to reach the shelter of the eaves before his clothes became thoroughly soaked.

Once he reached the front step, he took off his hat, beating the brim against the palm of his hand to shake off the raindrops and looked up at the dark clouds. Then he let himself into the narthex. He stood still for a moment, letting his eyes adjust to the dim interior.

His gaze went eagerly to the enormous curtains in the apse that covered the scaffolding, framing and stone work that had begun for the installation of the Holland window. His chest swelled with pleasure for the secret gift he was giving the people of Wellsey. The Earl had told him at that first meeting to "inspire them" and so, with this, he would!

This brief reverie was interrupted by a loud hiccup and a girlish sob.

Surprised for an instant, Christopher collected himself, and moved quickly towards the distressing sound. It was coming from the front of the nave. When he reached the top of the aisle, he found a young woman kneeling with her face buried in her hands, weeping.

Mr. Morton sank down next to her and waited for her to notice his presence, but she did not. She continued to sob. He quietly cleared his throat, and then, hesitating for a moment, reached out and patted her shoulder.

She sprang up. "Oh sir! Mr. Morton, it's you," she sniffled.

"Yes. What troubles you, Miss-?" His eyes widened when he recognized her. "Miss Prentice?"

"Aye, 'tis me," she responded miserably, sinking back down onto the pew.

Christopher waited for her to explain what pain had brought her at such an early hour alone to the church.

"Does the Lord care the same for women as he does men?" She asked, her pretty blue eyes, now reddened from stinging tears, lifted to his for a moment.

"Aye," he said, using her own soft, country expression. "The scriptures tell us that he cares about every sparrow that falls, and people are more important to Him than a little bird, surely; man, woman or child."

"That is good, then." She sniffled, "because I don't want God to be listening to my father more than He listens to me."

Christopher's brow creased sympathetically as he waited to hear her story.

"My mum is dead, you know," she began. "And I have got five young brothers and sisters to take care of. It's hard to keep them all fed, clean and clothed, you understand."

"I can imagine so, yes," he agreed.

"Well." here she started to cry a little harder as the words tumbled out. "My dad used to be a respected horseman, proper-like, but he-he lost our money at races. He couldn't stop hoping his luck would turn, so he kept going. And when Mum died, he took to drink. Now he keeps on me, telling me that I have got to get married, and soon, or he'll find someone for me to marry himself. His mind is addled, Mr. Morton!" Here she began to collapse into weeping. "We never would have come to this if Mum had lived."

"Miss Prentice," he sought to soothe her. "Your father is your father. I cannot think that he would wish you to be unhappy. He most likely wants what is best for you as well as your sisters and brothers. Do you have reason to fear his choice?"

"I do! Tis his old friend he's chosen! Mr. Bantry's practically my uncle!" she blushed fiercely, "Since I grew up, he looks at me in a funny way that makes me... uneasy."

Christopher wished he could refute what she said, and say that no such thing was likely, but he could not lie. Such sad things did occur, and frequently.

"How much time has your father given you?"

"By the end of harvest season, I need to have a pledge." Miss Prentice dissolved into tears once more.

Christopher wanted to comfort her, but his natural inclination to aid the troubled woman was tempered by his concern for propriety. "Let us pray and then I need to get to my study and you are needed at home. Perhaps God will provide you a husband or soften your father's heart."

Miss Prentice lifted her red-rimmed eyes and clutched her stomach. She shook once more and then nodded, "It will take a miracle, sir. Please help me ask for one?"

Christopher smiled at her consolingly, "Well, I would not say you need a miracle." He patted her hand encouragingly. "You are a kind and pretty girl and some bright young man will be happy to make you his wife."

This confidence brought a soggy smile from the young woman and she appeared to calm down considerably.

Christopher was struck suddenly with a mental image of Miss Prentice with Mr. Keevey, and he leaned forward eagerly and said with seriousness, "Miss Prentice. I may have an offer of marriage for you that would satisfy your father, but you must trust me." His parishioner blinked back tears and flushed pink anew as she gazed at him, hope and something else in her expression. "In the meantime, I could use your assistance with something," he continued. "Would you be willing to cook and clean a little, but mostly take care of two adorable children if I go with you myself to help my new friend, Mr. Keevey? I will make certain that you always have an escort for as long as it is necessary."

Miss Prentice nodded. "Aye. If you will go with me, I will go. I know Mr. Keevey."

"Of course," said Christopher, remonstrating with himself. "I am sure you know of him. Tell me, do you know what sort of a man Mr.

Keevey is, truly? For I confess I just met him, but I liked him in an instant. I want to understand if my reading of his character is accurate according to your better knowledge."

Again, she nodded and looked down. "His wife was a sweet woman and he treated her well. But she had the baby and died. Mrs. Purdy nursed the baby for a time, but now she must have given her back to her father." Miss Prentice stayed rosy under Christopher's scrutiny, and she glanced up just long enough to say, "I like babies, sir. If you want me to help Mr. Keevey, I will."

"Excellent! You may ride with me and one of my housemaids on Thursday and Monday until Mr. Keevey is well enough to take the man's share of labour up again and find a woman to help with the housework. Now, let us pray."

Christopher bowed his head and prayed a common prayer of blessing aloud, rising to a stand when he was finished. Miss Prentice held out her hand for assistance, which Christopher gave her. As soon as she was on her feet, he bowed his head to her politely and walked off to his study, leaving Miss Prentice to make her way to the door.

She did, but with a soft look in her eyes and a lightness in her step, for all her heavy skirts, that would have made the kindly vicar nervous if he had witnessed it.

That evening, he walked home slowly, his head filled with hopeful plans, not for his own happiness, which appeared unattainable, but for the potential singular solution to both Mr. Keevey's and Miss Prentice's difficulties. After crossing the church lawn, he paused for a moment on the footbridge to watch the early evening sun glinting upon the stream's surface and wet rocks, and then continued on his way.

Chapter Seven

Y ou are forcing me to go then?" asked Cherise woodenly.

"I would prefer you not think of it in just that way, but I suppose we are, yes," said her father, lifting his chin resolutely. He was a kind man, and generally liked to placate the women in his life rather than lord over them, but his wife would not be persuaded away from taking Cherise on a last outing before winter should set in. Lady Hamblin wished to take their daughter to London for the remainder of July and until the end of the Season or, as she had put it, "as long as it takes for Penfield or someone else acceptable to offer for her".

"But-" Cherise stretched out her hands as if she could see a table full of reasons not to go but could not articulate them. She put her fingertips to her temples. "I have so little notice! So little time to prepare! We leave tomorrow? Why, it is not fair!"

"It isn't fair, you say? Why ever not? Since when did pleasant surprises need permission from the receiver of them?" He closed his eyes for a moment and stroked his moustache.

"Oh, Father! I am sorry," said Cherise with feeling. "If you put it that way, I see what you must think of me, and I will try to be happy for your sake."

His eyes narrowed, "What exactly is it here in Cherrybrook that keeps you from wanting a short trip away? I must confess, this is new to me! You have never complained of adventure before, to my recollection."

Cherise stared wide-eyed at Lord Hamblin and realised that she had gone too far. She was more emotional than usual, and she desperately strove to stuff her unmanaged feelings out of sight once more. The truth of it was, that her mind had instantly procured an image of the packet of cherished letters which were tied with velvet ribbon and hidden in her bedroom. If she were swept off in this way, there would be no time to write to Mr. Morton to tell him where she was! He may believe her to be unfeeling, as if she had known for months that she was to leave, and neglected to tell him. Desperate to keep back a flood of tears, she pulled herself upright and tried to focus on the situation as her father saw it. He wanted her to be well-matched; to have experiences appropriate to her passion for art and living. Cherise made a grand effort to smile.

Her father's expression softened and he said gently, "There is my girl. I knew you would see the value in it." He turned to leave the room but before going he said, "I did not tell you earlier, my dear, for I meant it as a surprise, but I see now that perhaps that was not the best approach." His eyes twinkled and he tugged the ends of his moustache absentmindedly. " I have obtained tickets to the gallery. There are fine Roman pieces on exhibit, never before seen outside of that city and you, dearest, shall see them with your own eyes!"

"Oh Father, thank you!" Cherise rushed to her father and threw her arms about his neck and hugged him fiercely. She cried now, and her father could not possibly know what portion of the tears were from love and which from sadness. But nor could she.

Lord Hamblin pulled away from her embrace, and clapped his hands with a chuckle. "Now, get yourself up to your rooms and start the arduous task of choosing which gowns you shall take! You may acquire more in Town. I realise that you are being taken there to be seen and may be there for several weeks."

As Lord Hamblin had decreed, Cherise was rumbled away in the family's best carriage the next day, her mother across from her, reading the schedule she had made of all they were going to do, and who they were going to see. It was near the end of the Season, true, but it wasn't over yet, and it was oh, so fortunate that the Wesfords were there with rooms to spare.

"There are dances or parties at least two times a week, an opera, a garden tour and the art exhibit that you will adore, according to your father. You brought your paints?"

"Yes," answered Cherise. "You promised that we should go to the Palace Gardens and Hampton Court. How will you occupy yourself while I paint, I wonder? Did you bring your stitchery?"

"No, I shall have plenty to do with keeping you company and reading from time to time, I expect." Here her mother smiled a little. "Penfield will be in London as well. We are sure to meet him. It will be nice for you to have someone you recognise amongst the crowd."

"I hope you did not plan this trip merely to throw me in the path of the Viscount. I may meet him any day I please from home," said Cherise indignantly.

"I know you do not much care for him, but the familiarity might be comforting. Perhaps he has friends that he might introduce to us?"

Cherise stifled a groan and looked out the window. "I am too warm," she said decidedly. "Are you too warm as well, Mother?"

Her mother looked at Cherise through lowered eyelids and said calmly, "I am perfectly comfortable, thank you. I expect that I vexed you and got you all lighted up." Lady Hamblin inhaled deeply before continuing. "Cherise, I know you do not like it when I speak plainly about this, but you must understand that your father and I cannot keep dangling you in hopes that you will please someone suitable as much as they please you!" Here, her mother clasped her hands together beseechingly and tilted her elegant head. "I know how you have set your heart upon a match like your father and I, but you must realise by now that we are unusual; fortunate, but rare," her the corner of her mouth turned up slightly. "Why, most of my friends married proper gentlemen of agreeable rank and acceptable temper, and they have grown to admire, if not love, their husbands.

"Are you aware that you have had a full season, and this is our *third* stay in London? Oh, I do not know why I ask! Of course, you must have knowledge of it, but the sad part of it is that you don't care whether it is your third visit or not!" Lady Hamblin continued, her expression turning a trifle peevish. "Now we must come at the end or for a shorter stay so that we do not draw attention to how old you are becoming and how many times we have come in vain."

Cherise leaned forward in the carriage seat; her face flushed. "What about finding a husband that cares about my thoughts and talents?"

"What of them?" retorted her mother, also leaning forward. "Your talents will not make you a place in society the way marrying will. You see? This is why, even though I cannot say I find Lord Penfield to be entirely suited to you, he is well-known to us. Mark my words, you will run out of opportunities, Cherise, and soon!"

"Does Father know this is why you wanted to bring me?"

"He knows. We agreed that you have grown distracted of late and have turned... secretive. Spending too much time alone leads to self-ish and unsociable behaviours, unacceptable for a baron's daughter." Lady Hamblin picked at the tip of her glove and her voice rose a little as she tried to sound casual and said, "We have a responsibility to you, to our town." She sniffed. "You cannot wed an untitled man, Cherise. Your father and I will not allow it." She looked sharply at Cherise as if to see if her arrow had hit home. It had. Cherise sat back in her seat with a jump and while she held her chin high, she held her hands clenched tightly together and would not speak again unless it was absolutely necessary.

Being jostled about on the road had finished off what little spirit for argument that otherwise might have lingered, and so by the time they stopped at the inn that night, all attention and speech on the part of Lady Hamblin was dedicated to the practicalities and endless inconveniences of travel, which was met by a thick silence or at best, whispered replies on the part of her daughter.

It took long days of riding, shuffling in and out of coachyards and inns, before they arrived at her aunt and uncle's. Cherise dragged herself wearily up the front steps and waited like a piece of baggage for her mother and aunt to finish hugging and chattering. Her mother was the quieter and more elegant of the two sisters, warm but not embarrassingly so. Aunt Clara Wesford was the embarrassing sort, gushing, always speaking in superlatives and talking too much about trivial matters. Her husband, Mr. Jonathan Wesford, was a patient man who did not seem to mind or notice that his wife was a bit of a rattle.

When the older adults had finished greeting one another, they turned to Cherise. Aunt Clara fawned over her good looks and took her cheeks in her hands and shook Cherise's face a little, and said, "What a prize! We shall find you a husband this time. The richest young ladies are gone for the Season, engaged or married," said Clara aside to Cherise's mother before turning back to her niece. "You'll show up all the better in their absence. Several fine country squires will still be here, including your own Lord Penfield!" Aunt Clara twittered and giggled, raising her shoulders and covering her mouth as though she had said a very naughty thing. In Cherise's opinion, her aunt absolutely had.

Blessedly, Aunt Clara turned from this uncomfortable subject, and now she was talking to her sister about *this* dance and *that* party as they made their way into the tall, narrow house and up to their rooms to freshen up.

Cherise was grateful for the solitude given her and, after washing her face and hands, she curled up on the cushioned window seat of her room and stared unseeingly out the window. How was she to endure weeks of Town and Aunt Clara? She could not bear to consider Mr. Morton's reaction to her sudden departure. He would either believe that she had forgotten him or had willingly cast him off. Likely he would hear where she was by chance, through gossip. And there would be nothing he *would* do about it. There was nothing he *could* do about it, even if he wanted to. He spoke to her through his letters as one dear to him, but she could not be sure of the degree of his regard for her. He was entirely too well-behaved. She pressed her hand against her forehead, then with a sigh, stood to change out of her travelling clothes.

"Here you are. Here. You. Are," announced Lord Penfield to Cherise at the first occasion where they were contrived to meet. Hat in hand, his heavily-pomaded locks (cut in the Brutus mode) moved not a hair despite his vigorous, dipping bow. They had encountered one another in a crowded room, full of fringe members of the ton. Cherise wasn't foolish enough to believe they were otherwise. As her aunt had intimated, all the marriage mart "first prizes", those of the first stare, had already been carried off.

Cherise curtseyed automatically in response, and tried to look pleased to see him but not more than a cursory amount. It would not do to raise his hopes, if indeed he had any where she was concerned. Fortunately, she knew of just the topic to bring sobriety to their conversation.

"And how is your father, milord? Does he improve at all?"

"Oh, yes. I mean, no. No, he does no better, I am afraid. The doctor looks in on him frequently, and I am sent messages regularly. I don't suppose he'll last the month out."

Cherise scowled. "Then, why are you here?" she asked impertinently.

"Why, my father takes no notice of me whether I am there or not. In fact, I think I annoy him. A good man, the best kind, but the stiff, old sort- you know what I mean? He has no use for the young."

"You can hardly be considered young--" she began, but Lady Hamblin, who was now listening with more attention, overheard this, and pulled Cherise by the arm to silence her.

Cherise was surprised that Lord Penfield had even recognized that he was being insulted. He pulled his head back and considered her more carefully, then said with a predatory grin, "As I recall, you are not many years behind me. You must soon be running out of eligible suitors."

Lady Hamblin gave a nervous laugh then, with birdlike movements, looked between her daughter and their neighbour and said in a sing-song voice, "We have come here for the art exhibition, Lord Penfield." She smiled sweetly, "Why, my sister kindly procured invitations to soirees and dances, but we are here for *art*. My husband says that anyone who is anyone ought to see the *Marbles*."

Cherise nodded in agreement, daring to look askance at the Viscount. "You know about it of course?" She asked, raising an eyebrow, "You told me that you had been to Rome and Greece for the art, but now the continent has come to us, and father wouldn't let me miss it for the world." This proved a fitting distraction for he was reminded of events from his own recent escapades.

"Ah yes," he said, throwing his head back. "*Such* a time I had on my tour. I was there only last summer, you know." The way he patted his stomach affectionately when he said it made Cherise think that he must have indulged his appetites rather too well in Rome. He went on. "This year I was in Paris, or I would not be coming to Town so late, you see. I missed the fullest part of the Season here, but no matter-"

"You have been here several seasons," she reminded him with a smile, but this time Lord Penfield was ready for Cherise's parry, "as have I," she added to placate him. The trick was in putting him off without openly offending him or her mother.

Lord Penfield's attention was suddenly stolen by a youngish man who had just entered the room. Penfield waved and held up a finger for the fellow to wait for him. Then, turning back to Cherise, he said, "Miss Hamblin, pray excuse me. I am buying a real goer from that chap and need to make some arrangements." He looked away distractedly and then back at her. "Please, would you honour me with the first turn about the room at Lady Metcalf's dance next week? You are invited, yes?"

Whether he meant to catch her not having been invited to Lady Metcalf's, or whether he actually wished to dance with her, was unknown to Cherise. Regardless of the reason, with her mother hanging over her shoulder with owl-like intensity, Cherise bowed her head and curtseyed in acquiescence. Anything to see him walk away and leave her alone.

Day after day dragged by in this manner, with Cherise upbraiding herself in private for allowing herself to have fostered an affection for Mr. Morton, who would never ask for her. Yet, she could not deny that she found all the available men (who were her social equals) to be shallow, unattractive, and dull. The only bright spot of that month was the few days she was able to haul about her painting kit and do her best to capture the extraordinary views of Hampton Court gardens and their promised visit to the National Gallery in the newly-named Trafalgar Square.

To step into a building dedicated to some of the best art that man had wrought! Those worlds that could be contained in a room or on a wall moved Cherise to tears of admiration and profound pleasure. She couldn't explain to herself why she felt the way she did. It seemed to her that her happy and sad moods entwined in the presence of masterful art.

Her heart raced and her eyes sparkled as she stood before one piece after glorious piece. She would enter a gallery room and stand in the doorway, glancing about the space. Always one or several artworks would jump to her attention and she would make her way to stand before them and soak in what she could. Sometimes it was the story represented in the painting or sculpture that intrigued her, and sometimes it was the technical mastery that left her in awe.

It wasn't the dark pieces that stole her heart, it was the colourful, light ones. There were new historical paintings by David Wilkie that, while they told stories not long past about the victories at Waterloo, had been painted with a poetic touch, like that of the Venetian painters. The skies were alive with clouds that seemed to move, the trees swayed and the colours and composition of the figures and animals made them appear as though they lived and breathed in the scenes.

There were enormous, wildly colourful paintings of modern scenes by William Turner, great, slashing works that embodied the power of nature versus man's strongest ships and cities.

She was also drawn to the small, jewel-like portraits of women, sometimes the Madonna, sometimes saints or queens, all painted with care and control. The choices of delicate and juxtaposed vibrant colours were painted with a brush so fine, even an individual eyelash was discernible.

Finally, with a shaking hand, Cherise gave her special ticket to the sculpture exhibit to the gallery guard and heard her mother do the same behind her.

They stood side by side in the archway. Before them was a room of marble bodies and busts from the heart of Rome. Many of the classical works were instantly recognisable to Cherise. But while the exposed bodies writhing in pleasure or pain was shocking, the passion and masterful artistry kept Cherise from averting her eyes although she knew she blushed.

What impressed Cherise most, was how soft the flesh looked, how finely the hair was wrought, or how delicately the grape leaf vines serpentined around the figures, although all was made of stone.

She watched furtively as a young married couple walked around the room together, A couple of times they leaned in close to whisper something to one another, and the wife would giggle.

"I cannot believe your father thought this a suitable exhibit," sniffed her mother, rummaging through her reticule for her vinaigrette. "It is not at all the thing for a well-bred female."

"It is *Art*, Mamma," said Cherise with an inaudible sigh. "but we can go back to the painting gallery if you prefer." Lady Hamblin needed no second invitation. She turned around quickly and marched out of the sculpture gallery; back to the safety of the paintings. Cherise left the exhibit more slowly, looking boldly about her one last time before going in search of her mother.

Back in the pictures part of the gallery, Cherise was grateful that her mother allowed her plenty of time to absorb what she saw. As long as there was nothing which could be considered objectionable, Lady Hamblin was patient. *Still,* Cherise couldn't help thinking, *It would have been nice to have come here with someone who loved art as much as she did. Someone like Mr. Morton.*

How he would exclaim over the perfection collected here! He would love the drawings, even though most of them were unfinished "cartoni", merely preparatory sketches for an artist's more ambitious work. In addition to Mr. Morton, she supposed her father might enjoy it. The thing was, her father was always in such a hurry! He would rush about and conquer it, as might Lord Penfield. And the annoying Penfield would doubtlessly say "how remarkable, how remarkable," without remembering any particular piece strongly enough to remark upon it afterwards!

Lady Hamblin and Cherise strolled around the galleries until they were weak with hunger, then made their way to the exit. Cherise was so happy to have been permitted to see the exhibitions that it nearly made up for the less savoury parts of her London stay. That was, as long as she could hold off any serious suitors and keep Lord Penfield at bay. She wondered how long her mother intended to keep her here...

Chapter Eight

I t seemed to Christopher that the first visit to the Keeveys with
Miss Prentice had gone well. Oh, there had been frightfully few
words exchanged, and shyness all around, but that was to be expected
and even commended. It simply meant that the participants were as
well-behaved and as proper as he had hoped.

He'd driven over with one of his own housemaids, a strong but
quiet woman named Mrs. Lowell, whom Thea had described as a
first-rate soldier in the war against dust and disorder.

They had left the vicarage immediately following breakfast, stopping to pick up Eliza Prentice on their way. Miss Prentice and Mrs.
Lowell started out quietly enough, but after a few minutes Mrs. Lowell began clucking over the sadness of Keevey on account of his losing
his missus, and the harrowing adventures that must surely have been
his lot as a widower with two little ones, girls no less. Eliza began to
relax and soon chimed in, wondering aloud what vignettes of disorder
the pair might discover upon arrival. It was to be Miss Prentice's task to
spend most of her time with the children, washing them and cooking

for them as might be needed, whilst Mrs. Lowell would handle the rest of the washing and the cleaning.

Christopher could tell that (since his previous visit) Mr. Keevey had put some little effort into tidying and taking care of the worst of the messes. Neither Mrs. Lowell nor Miss Prentice seemed put off by what they found when the man of the house welcomed them inside.

Miss Prentice wasted no time in taking possession of Lucy. She pried the baby gently from her father's arms and headed toward the kitchen, encouraging Martha to follow close and assist with her sister. Both girls stared at this cheerfully commanding intruder with wide eyes and straight mouths, but they did not cry.

When the young ones had gone, Mrs. Lowell asked where she could find the laundry and the mending. And, when she got her bearings, she grunted dismissively at the men and rolled up her sleeves. Christopher, rightly comprehending her desire to work alone, asked Mr. Keevey what he might like done out-of-doors.

Instead of answering, Keevey moved slowly towards the doorway to the kitchen, careful to stay out of both women's' lines of sight. A smile crept slowly over his face. Christopher attributed the man's good humour to the fatherly pleasure of hearing no tearful outbursts, only his daughters' contented voices and the comforting sound of Miss Prentice's soothing chatter.

Mr. Keevey must have been satisfied with how well introductions had gone, for suddenly he smoothed back his hair and moved towards the door, grinning at Christopher. "You ready, then?"

With his able arm, he took a battered hat from a high hook. He apparently had every intention of joining Christopher in the fields and barn.

Because both of the women were accustomed to seeing at a glance what needed to be done, the day went by without incident and much was accomplished. When the lunch dishes had been cleared, and Miss Prentice had gotten a nice roast chicken set in the oven for the Keeveys' dinner, it was time to return to Wellsey. Christopher brought the carriage around to the front door of the cottage where the others stood waiting.

Mr. Keevey smiled warmly when Christopher took his hand, and the little girls hugged in close to their father, just as they had the first time he had caught sight of them. Looking at Mr. Keevey, Christopher thought the anxious lines around his new friend's mouth and eyes had eased a bit today.

After the ladies had finished bidding the happily huddled family goodbye, the Keeveys began to move back to the front steps while Christopher hopped into the carriage. He reached down to pull up a basket of mending before extending his hand to help Mrs. Lowell.

When it was Miss Prentice's turn, he discovered the young woman was staring up at him with shining eyes and her hand outheld. She looked inordinately eager to have Christopher take her hand and pass her up into the carriage. He fervently hoped the excited glow in her eyes and cheeks had nothing to do with himself.

She scooted back onto the seat and they set off down the drive. The way Miss Prentice spoke, scarcely taking time to breathe between her anecdotes of the little girls, seemed to suggest to Christopher that her apparent eagerness to leave wasn't, he hoped, so much that she had been in a hurry to ride home with him, but that she was fit to burst with the need to talk about her experiences at the Keeveys'. By the time they had turned onto the main road by the broken fence, Christopher felt justified in dismissing the worst of his fears.

Miss Prentice inhaled deeply and continued, "... And I could not carry little Lucy and the puppy at once, you see, so Martha carried the dog and although it was nearly as big as she was, she had one hand under its bottom to support it and the other hand grasping the pup by the scruff of the neck. No matter how it twisted and licked, she did not drop it! It may not seem like much to you or me, but for a child as young as Martha is, it shows that she is an observant and responsible little person."

"How does it show that she is observant?" Christopher quizzed.

"Why, she must have watched her father handle the dogs and learnt from him to support them from the bottom."

"Ah! And how does it show that she is responsible?"

"Because she did not drop it!" She flashed him a smile.

Christopher chuckled at her answer and let her continue to talk. Already she seemed to have developed an affection for the two motherless girls, which was no less than he had hoped for.

Each time they rode back to town, it seemed that Miss Prentice had more to say than the last time, if that were possible, but Christopher did not discourage her talking as it seemed to bring her immense pleasure, something the young woman very much needed.

It had been five weeks since he had last heard from Miss Hamblin, and even though his mother had returned home from her sister's house,

Christopher still felt alone somehow. Part of him was missing, and he suspected that part was a tender piece of his heart.

Once, in a state of despondency, he had taken a small watercolour set and a handful of brushes with him to The Artist's Folly. For the first while, he simply sat where she used to sit, staring out across the water. When he had at last worked up the nerve to try painting, he could almost be grateful that it had started to rain. The colour mixes he had were dull, and if anything, the raindrops which pelted his painted grey sky improved the effect. It was a failed attempt to find colour in this place without Cherise, he thought bitterly as he put up his umbrella. Christopher dumped out the contents of his water jar and packed up his things. When he was part of the way home, the clouds cleared and the sun emerged once more, but he did not stop to try again. He took the paints and brushes home and slid them into a drawer.

Another day, Christopher stared at the ground as he hurried along the pitted streets of Wellsey, lost in thought. He had told himself that as long as Miss Hamblin was well, as long as she was happy, that was all that mattered, but he longed to hear from her.

The worst of it was, he could not enquire openly about her without arousing interest or censure. Reverend Lyle, the vicar at Cherrybrook, had mentioned nothing. Mrs. Terrence, whom he knew to be a great friend of Lady Hamblin's, also offered nothing. For the first time in his life as a minister, Christopher visited his parishioners actually hoping for gossip!

With furrowed brows and long strides, he walked briskly through the town and only when he had come to the end of a row of shops, and had turned the corner, did he remember why he had come. He took out his watch and flicked it open. Seeing it was not too late to take care of the matter, he changed direction. He stepped back into the main street and, glancing down inopportunely at his pocket as he replaced his watch, he collided with some force into Miss Prentice, who was carrying a large basket on her hip.

She stumbled a little and hauled herself up, looking embarrassed.

Christopher stopped in surprise and swept off his hat. "Miss Prentice, I *do* apologise," he faltered. "My mind was wandering and I am in too much of a hurry for my own good... and yours, too, apparently! Are you hurt?" he inquired solicitously.

"Oh no, sir," the young woman said, shaking her golden-haired head. She glanced up at him and said quickly, before he could move off, "Oh, please don't go yet, Mr. Morton!" She lurched forward as though to catch his sleeve but thought the better of it at the last second. She steadied herself and moved the basket to her other hip. "I wonder, have you called upon Mrs. Carls this week?" She asked shyly.

"No," he answered with concern, "but I will visit today if you recommend I do so. Is there something I ought to know?"

She looked down for a moment before continuing, "Mrs. Carls can no longer get out of her bed and... and, well, I have just come from her place. I've been cleaning there."

Truly, Miss Prentice was a ministering angel, he thought. Christopher blinked slowly and said, "I will look in on her then. Once again you impress me with your kindness, Miss Prentice."

"It gets me out of my own place and away from my father," she reminded him. After a moment's hesitation, she added, "He came for supper again last night. My father's friend." She stood still, looking up at him imploringly.

Christopher pinched the bridge of his nose. Recently, he had begun to wonder if, by his offer to assist her, that she had misunderstood his intentions. She couldn't believe that he had been suggesting *himself* as a marriage prospect, could she? She couldn't! And yet... he groaned inwardly and forced his mind to turn from that course and said, " I have not forgotten your predicament, Miss Prentice, and I urge you to remain calm and strong. For my own part, I wholeheartedly believe that you will have an acceptable offer in time to satisfy your father."

"I hope you are right, Mr. Morton." She looked him full in the face and he saw how hopeful she looked. How she trusted him. It was coming to the final edge of her faith.

"I will see you in church?" he asked, his voice sounding distant and not quite like his own.

"Aye," she responded with a nod, her deep blue eyes never leaving his face.

"All right then. Do not lose heart, Miss Prentice."

Miss Prentice looked down, her lashes damp. She bowed her head and Christopher heard her say with feeling, "Thank you, sir," as she adjusted the basket more comfortably upon her hip and set off. As he watched her go, the thought crossed his mind that her burden seemed to have lessened, whilst his had grown.

As soon as Christopher looked away from Miss Prentice to proceed on his way, he was spotted by the Kent sisters. However unpleasant they may be, they were residents of Cherrybrook, and today that fact made his pulse quicken. If anyone had news of Cherise, it would be the Kents. He plucked his hat from his head and bowed as the women approached.

"Good day, ladies."

"Why, Mr. Morton, how we have missed you! Are you and your mother well?"

"Yes, quite well. And your family?"

"We are all in fine health," said Teresa (or was it Angela?). She had her orb-like eyes fixed on him whilst her sister squinted down the street at the retreating form of Miss Prentice. "Mrs. Terrence tells us that your mother was away visiting her sister and getting some much-needed rest. Has she now returned home?"

"She has," replied Christopher. "And I do believe she is better for having gone. It is not so much that she has been feeling unwell, but that seeing her sister boosted her spirits."

"Poor spirits invite poor health. That is what Mamma always says," interjected Angela (or was it Teresa?) who was still craning her neck to watch the passers-by. Any harboured hope that his private conversation with Miss Prentice would be ignored set sail when he saw the sisters exchange glances. The first one silently mouthed, *"Eliza Prentice"* to the other, and they smiled smugly in unison and then looked up, wide-eyed, waiting to be addressed again. Christopher could feel his throat tighten with annoyance.

Of all the people to have seen him stop and talk with Miss Prentice, the Kents were the worst. Everyone in Wellsey and Cherrybrook would hear it whispered behind a glove within a day or two.

"Thank you for your concern." His jaw twitched. "I will be sure and tell my mother that you inquired after her." He glanced about, hoping to see Mr. or Mrs. Kent but he did not. "Someone must be expecting you. I will not keep you from either your tasks or your social engagements."

"We are on our way to pay a call on Mrs. Terrence whilst Father pays his respects to the Earl."

"Ah. I am afraid your father's thoughtful call will be in vain," he warned them. "Naturally, Mr. Wilcox or a footman will be happy to deliver a message to the Earl. Besides his son, the household staff and the doctor, I am the only one that his lordship will see."

The ladies put their heads near one another and looked up at him, "He must be that poorly now! Has anyone been sent to inform the Viscount? Lord Penfield is in Town you know. He and Miss Hamblin are often seen together." Was it his imagination or were the sisters staring unblinkingly at him, watching for a visceral reaction? The twitch in his jaw worsened.

Christopher feigned indifference to their news, and stated simply that he trusted the staff of Penfield House to inform the Viscount when the doctor said it was imperative to do so. It was not the Kents' business to hear from him how near death the Earl might be, and he had learned more than he had wished to know about Cherise. Unwilling to spend a moment longer than necessary in their company, he nodded and lifted his hat. "Please, give my regards to your parents," he said. And he took his leave.

As the morning sunlight filtered through the curtains of his room, Christopher opened his eyes with effort, and stretched his arms over his head. His sleep had been short and troubled.

Cherise was in Town, then. There was only one reason he could think of for an unattached baron's daughter to be taken there, and that was to obtain a husband. Christopher had come to understand Miss Hamblin well enough through her letters, that he knew any such pressure would gall her. And, if Lord Penfield was dangling after her, as the Kents implied he was, then a marriage proposal from that quarter was not out of the question.

Although he was a man, healthy, strong, and therefore privileged, Christopher felt himself bound nearly as much as a woman must be in that aspect of life that mattered as much as anything could: matrimony. It was not putting it too strongly to say that beyond a living, the wedded state would contribute more to life's joys than anything else.

During the darkest hours of the morning, this thought had led him to consider the lessons of Samson. That young prophet had been betrayed by his eyes and body. In repentance, it became his duty to God and his people to sacrifice his desires, to mortify that traitorous flesh for the lives of his family and community.

It seemed to Christopher there was no possibility that he would ever be able to court Miss Hamblin, and though he stopped short of comparing Miss Hamblin to Samson's Delilah, he believed he loved Cherise, and the only honourable ways forward were to openly court her, or to stop all communication between them. Miserably, he realised that he had not had the satisfaction of seeing his heart's desire above five times in person, yet through their letters he felt sure her passion and opinions matched his own. She wrote openly of their shared love of art, the natural world and their neighbours, with a sensitivity and humour that captivated him. And whenever they met, it was like no other meeting. There was a force that drew them together, compelled them to talk, to touch, to want more from the other than anyone else. At least that is how it was for him. Restraint was an ever-increasing torment.

Of course, she was beautiful. She possessed a quiet, even intimidating beauty. She was ladylike in all ways, perhaps excepting the honesty and directness of her conversation. But then it had struck him from the beginning, that that particular generosity was only for a favoured few.

And now she had gone without giving him the honour of an explanation. Even if she had not wished to go, surely she would have informed him of her plans? He recalled the evening dinner party at Penfield House. She had feigned a flirtation with the Viscount and it had annoyed him at the time, but he comprehended that for her to insult Lord Penfield openly would have been to throw away the only acceptable husband close to home.

He ran his fingers through his hair, pulling through the tangles ruthlessly. He had no right whatsoever to demand any civility, any affection from her, for he could deserve none. From the first handshake with her father and bow to her mother at the Soldiers' Dance, he knew he could have no important place in her life.

After finishing with his usual preparations for the day, he stepped out into the hall and encountered Thea carrying a tray toward his mother's room. Having expected to find his mother in the morning room, this was unusual. With a perfunctory knock at his mother's door, Christopher ushered Thea ahead into the room.

"Here's Thea with your morning tea, Mother," he announced. Mrs. Morton was sitting up, leaned against a short wall of pillows, her nightcap neatly in place, and her blankets made around her very tidily, as if she had planned to entertain from her bed.

"You overslept?" She glanced in his direction as she received the tray. Christopher noticed there were two cups on the tray; his mother had been expecting him.

"I will pour, Thea. Thank you," said his mother. Neither he nor she spoke until the maid had gone from the room and softly closed the door.

"How are you feeling?" Christopher asked with concern.

"I think these packets from the doctor do nothing, but I will give them more time to work. What else can I do?" she smiled weakly at him. "Please, sit down," said his mother with a nod. "How is the Earl, have you heard? Is he worsening?" Her expression was unreadable.

"He is," sighed Christopher as he lowered himself into the indicated chair next to her bed. "I expect the cough will carry him away any day now. And, although he has been extraordinarily strong to have withstood it all this time, I believe after reading to him this week, that he has lost his will to live, and lingers only in this twilight for days, if not hours."

"Has the Viscount been called home?" His mother picked up the teapot and began pouring the steaming water over the fragrant blend, her hand trembling slightly.

"Not that I am aware of," said Christopher. "I will call at Penfield House today and ask if there have been any changes. The doctor is expected tomorrow. If he sends a message to Lord Penfield, we can hope that he heeds the warning and comes home in time to pay his respects to his father."

His mother said nothing more about Lord Stafford, but only stared out the window, and when Christopher looked to see what she gazed upon, he saw nothing but the trees swaying in the gentle wind. A single leaf floated down from a tree whose top was hidden up and out of sight. Christopher cleared his throat and meant to speak, but his mother stopped him.

"Something has happened, Christopher, and I cannot like it, but neither can I ignore it." She looked up at him with an eyebrow lifted. "Mrs. Stiles delivered some shop goods yesterday afternoon. Sometimes she lets drop news of local interest that you as a man and a vicar are not privy to." Here his mother paused but did not reach for her teacup, instead she stared steadily at him. "Mrs. Stiles told me that Miss Prentice has hinted to her, and goodness knows how many other tradespeople," she added under her breath, "that you have indicated a partiality for her. It was all I could do to maintain decorum! Of course, I refuted the tale, for surely you would have shared such a notion with me if you had entertained it.

"I have asked you to look around you, I know." Spots of colour appeared on her cheekbones and forehead. "You should marry, yes, but not in haste!" Her voice was tense with emotion. "It would please me to see you settle and begin your domestic life, but I cannot imagine that you would have chosen Eliza Prentice! She is a sweet child, I know, but whatever would you talk about? You are self-sacrificing, Christopher, too much so, I believe. To marry so unequally where education, interest and conversation are concerned is outside acceptability! Please tell me that I did right by correcting the record in no uncertain terms with Mrs. Stiles?" Mrs. Morton sat up straight as an arrow and became agitated when Christopher was slow to answer her.

At first he sat frozen, listening in stunned silence, then he sat back with a thump in the chair and looked up at the ceiling, closing his eyes for a full minute, waiting for something. Holy intervention? He knew not what. He heard nothing. At last with a sigh, he leaned forward again and met his mother's gaze.

He swallowed hard before speaking. "I -I do not desire, *not at all*, to marry Miss Prentice for the very reasons you have stated but, hold fast to your charity, for she is a good girl with a troublesome father. You know of him, I expect? A sad piece, more often drunk than sober. Miss Prentice has been in charge of their household since the death of his wife, but he has another, younger daughter that will take Miss Prentice's place when she marries." He sighed deeply. "The man means to see Miss Eliza marry to lighten his load. Fewer mouths to feed this winter, perhaps?" Christopher sat quietly for a moment, staring at the rug. He made a stifled growl of frustration, and held his head in his hands, "How could I have been so idiotish." He mumbled, "I have begun congratulating myself for having found the girl a husband, but now I will confess to you that I have sometimes thought she showed a fancy for me, in the beginning."

Mrs. Morton grew more animated and spoke quickly. "'In the be-ginning'? My dearest, this was told to me yesterday! It is not your place to rescue the girl, for hers is a plight more than one country girl faces. For now she has gone and told more than one matron in town that you promised to find her a husband, and what are busybodies expected to think, other than you might be referring to yourself? Is this true?

Christopher squeezed his eyes shut and pinched the bridge of his nose.

"I must speak to Miss Prentice... I must make it clear."

"Christopher!" her voice wobbled.

He looked up and spoke evenly, with a firm voice, one not easily flown against. "She is a naive girl, Mother, and cannot have understood what damage she might do to us by her careless talk. You must know that I did not intend for Miss Prentice to feel as though I had singled her out, or in any way favoured her as a man might do, but I did give her hope of a proposal of marriage."

His mother leaned forward in mild alarm and choked. "Christopher... I have always felt some anxiety that your strength of character may lead you to marry beneath you." She reached out to touch his hand. "Please, promise me that you will not offer for any woman without first confiding in me."

Christopher laughed mirthlessly. "I have very few choices. You needn't worry yourself."

"But not Miss Prentice, surely?"

"No, Mother. You mistake me." Christopher stood up and rested his arm along the mantelpiece and gazed unseeingly down at the grate. He gave a dry laugh. "Can you see me, Mother, in the role of match-maker?" Christopher looked back at her with a wry smile.

His mother raised questioning eyes to his, as he continued; "You are already acquainted with Eliza Prentice, but you have not, to my knowledge, met Mr. Keevey."

Christopher described the man and his situation to his mother, and finished by telling her, "I have been to see Keevey, and confirmed that he is not at all opposed to making a proposal of marriage to Miss Prentice... quite eager, in fact. It would be an excellent match for both of them, as well as for the little ones. But I can see it is important that I create distance between myself and Miss Prentice, so that she has time to notice the man and marriage prospect that is under her very nose." He paused, and looked at his mother consideringly. "Would you be willing to take my place twice a week in driving Miss Prentice and Mrs.

Lowell to Keevey's farm? He is able now to take care of most of his former tasks but, as his friend, I will pay him a call soon to make sure of it."

Mrs. Morton sat up straighter and then said miffishly, "You know you needn't ask when you know the answer."

"Your health, though, Mother. Are you....?"

"Yes. Anyway, I feel remarkably stronger after hearing what you have said." She smiled, one side of her mouth turned up more than the other, and her mood seemed to have brightened. She stirred her tea, rather vigorously, Christopher thought. Then she said in a light, careless tone, "Is there any news of Lady and Miss Hamblin?"

Christopher felt his jaw twitch with suppressed emotion and forced himself to unclench his teeth. *Why must his mother remind him of Miss Hamblin?* He knew he was in danger of giving her an angry response, so best to keep it short. "The heart can be a dangerous governor, Mother. It cannot be trusted. Even if every correct feeling were there, that lady can never be mine. To answer your question, Miss Hamblin is in London, as she should be, and has been seen more than once, I gather, on the arm of Lord Robert Penfield."

Before his mother could ask him any more questions or break down his resolve to remain calm, he stood tall and came near, dropping a kiss on her forehead. He patted her hand reassuringly, and said, "Do not fret yourself. I will do the right thing for all of us." And with that, he hastily left the room.

Not an hour later, Christopher was in his study, carefully drafting a letter.

"Dear Friend,

I trust you are well and doing your utmost to enjoy the delights particular to Town.

I do not blame you for not informing me of your departure, for one of these three encumbrances might have kept you from it.

The first might be that your letter was intercepted by a passing wanderer or a particularly large bird (we know how they can be). The second is that you were whisked away suddenly and had no time to write, then trudge over the field to leave it here (was it raining that week? I cannot remember having marked it, but then again, I did not know you were gone). The third is that you understood then, as I do now, that it would do no good to inform me one way or the other, for sadly it changes nothing.

Whatever news you bring, I am determined to think it the best of news if you believe it so. Autumn always brings change.

Yours etc.,

A Friend"

When he had finished, he folded it carefully and stuck it in his pocket, gathered up his pencils and paper, and strode off toward the pond. He tried to sing as he walked, but when every song that came to mind was morbid or a ballad with a grim ending, he left off trying, and let the hum and buzz of insects and the bird songs uplift his spirits if they could.

Christopher reached the oak tree where he had first stood and observed Cherise painting all those months ago. It felt like a sacred place and he stepped carefully, as if he might unwittingly tread on a memory and destroy it forever. When he sat down on Cherise's log, for it was always her log to him, he stroked the worn, polished wood with his fingers. The wood was smooth, elegantly curved, and unpretentious, just like the lady. He started when a flock of birds swooped through the clearing, and he smiled a little as he pulled his pencil box into his lap. Before sharpening his drawing pencils with the little pocketknife he had with him, he fished the folded letter from his pocket and wedged it into the hollow of the log. He wondered how long it would remain hidden there before she found it. His heart cried out for her return, but his mind warned him that it was perhaps better she should stay away. For if she were absent long enough, the gossip about Miss Prentice might dissipate or better yet, be decently covered up by church banns for Eliza and Mr. Keevey.

He played out the scene in his mind. He would wait until he knew that she had returned to Cherrybrook, and add four or five days to it, time enough for her to come once to the pond. He would give her a period within which to respond to his letter. Or no, perhaps it would be best to tell her the story himself; tell her that it had all been a misunderstanding. That course of action, he decided, was a selfish impulse on his part, because he could offer no proposal that she would be allowed to accept. The longer that they carried on this secret friendship, the longer he kept her from being a gentleman's proper spouse and moving on with life.

But perhaps Cherise really did consider him only a friend? Was it possible? She might, this very minute in fact, be talking, walking, or even dancing with some titled gentleman or even Penfield. Christopher frowned deeply at such an eligible, yet unhappy, match.

With effort, he forced his worries aside and began to study and draw the outcropping of the tree roots that were in front of him as he sat looking out toward the water. He tilted his head to the right and left, trying to capture the grace of the lines. Finally, he was resolved to call the drawing finished. It was as he saw it; a tangle of roots that still were beautiful in their way, if only one had the right frame of mind to see it.

"It is from Louisa!" she declared in some excitement. Lady Hamblin sank, almost without looking, into a chair in the morning room of Aunt Clara's as she scanned the contents of her latest letter. Cherise sat across from her, nibbling toast.

"Does she have news of his lordship's health?"

"No." Suddenly, her mother stiffened.

"Then what is it, Mother? You have such a peculiar look upon your face."

"Incredible!" she exclaimed, laying the letter down onto her lap and picking it up again. "There has been a most shocking rumour! *Quite* shocking. No, it is not the Earl. It is the vicar!"

Cherise gasped and stared at her mother.

"It is on every local's tongue that a young woman named Eliza Prentice has made it known that she has received marked attention from Mr. Morton! Louisa says that if there is to be a marriage ahead, it will generally be understood to be either out of pity or indiscretion. The entire town is buzzing with the news, and Louisa herself does not know who to listen to. Apparently, she heard of it from Mrs. Kent! Then she goes on to say that Wellsey ought not to suffer moral paucity in its minister, and I quite agree. Can you imagine any tale so scandalous adhering to our own Cherrybrook vicar?"

"Mother," said Cherise censoriously, "our Reverend Lyle is the father of four children, the oldest of whom is just about to be married.

I hardly think your analogy is an apt one." She paused and rushed on, "He must have his reasons."

"Who must have his reasons? Mr. Morton, you mean?"

"Yes, Mr. Morton."

"Are you defending him?"

"I doubt he needs my defence. I am only saying that we should not rush to judge. For myself, I can well imagine the prodigious amount of tittle-tattle that such a matter must elicit, but it might be explained away very easily tomorrow."

Cherise forced herself to nibble the bits of breakfast that still remained, conscious of her mother's scrutiny. She tried to stay serene on the outside, but inside, a flood of wretched, sickening emotions were sweeping through her. "All I mean to say is; it is not seemly for ladies to become too excited by sensational news until it has been confirmed."

Her mother lowered her eyelids and blinked slowly at Cherise. "You cannot doubt when and if banns will be read, child. There will be nothing more to say at that time, but until then... I confess that I am not surprised to hear of some scandal or other involving Mr. Morton. He is too wealthy, mysterious, and attractive not to have fallen prey to a fortune-hunting female, but to be snared by one with so little to bring to a marriage! That is shocking indeed! He should have been more careful. Obviously, his mother did not warn him sufficiently.

"I am thankful that your father and I have had no reason to fear such imprudent behaviour from you." Seeing the effect her words had upon her daughter, Mrs. Hamblin faltered, "Are you quite well, Cherise? You have taken this news more to heart than I would have expected. What are the Mortons' concerns to you?"

"Nothing, really," Cherise lied. "It is only that I believe Mrs. Morton and her son to be well-bred people, to understand the way of things, but indeed, *if* the banns are read, you will be correct. There will be nothing more to say in such a case. That is all. Excuse me now, I am finished with my breakfast and I want to write to Phoebe."

"Very well, I will see you at dinner," said her mother without looking up.

Cherise stood shakily to walk, her feet felt heavy, as if she were wearing boots of lead as she left the room and sought solitude. Gratefully, she met no one in the hall or on the stairs. Her silent tears would have been hard to explain away. Once she had quietly closed the door behind her, she leaned her back against the wood, pinching her eyes shut in an effort to stop the tears. She had no right to them.

After a few minutes of struggle, she gained mastery over her unruly emotions and pushed herself to a weary stand, crossing the room to a small table and chair. Lowering herself into the chair, she took a deep breath and rested her cheek in her hand, staring out the window. She watched a small flock of finches race in small loops, squawking and trying to peck at one of their own. Finally, the lone bird shot off, escaping far enough away to where the others decided it was not worth the chase. They had won.

Cherise sighed. She would take her own advice and do her utmost to remain neutral until she heard something substantive, preferably from Mr. Morton himself.

With this resolve, she forced herself to write to her cousin as she had told her mother she would. When she was finished, she pulled a clean sheet of paper from her wooden lap desk and began a second letter of selfless congratulations to Mr. Morton. Even if she never had a cause to give it to him, it would feel good to write out her feelings.

It took a long time for the thoughts and words to form. She wanted him to know that she still held him in high regard, and that she understood that he must have an excellent reason for marrying Miss Prentice. She told him discreetly that she cared for him enough to let him go. When she was finished, she folded the paper, creasing the fold with the back of her fingernail. Then she rose and crossed the room to her paint box and hid the note inside it. She nestled it carefully alongside the letter she had written weeks ago about her favourite story. She had not had time to deliver it before leaving for London.

Her head throbbed. If she were home, she might have taken to the fresh air for a reviving walk, but here in the confines of London, her only option was to remove her shoes, curl up on the bed, and press a pillow tightly to her aching heart.

Today became yesterday many times over, and every time that Christopher managed to get to the willow pond, he found only his own folded letter. After several days of incessant rain in September he gently fished out the lodged note, carefully unfolding it to be sure it was in his own handwriting. It was, only now it had softened and the ink had faded. Feeling downcast, he tore the paper into soggy pieces and wadded them into a small, damp ball and threw them into the water. He did not permit himself to write another letter, but he came to The Artist's Folly from time to time to read a book or draw in the privacy of the willows.

Christopher heard nothing more about Cherise, and now it was well past the London social season. He wondered what kept the Hamblins away and why the Viscount did not return home. Hunting, by now, was in full swing and small towns like Cherrybrook and Wellsey were crowded with the peers' set, expensive jumpers, and baying dogs. It made no sense to Christopher. However, for one reason he was exceedingly grateful that Cherise's return had been delayed.

His mother had made good her offer to assist Christopher in driving Miss Prentice to Keevey's farm, and Christopher was able to avoid that damsel (with the exception of church) throughout several weeks. However, one wet day, as he rode out of Wellsey to pay a call, he happened upon Miss Prentice. She was trudging along the muddy roadside, the inevitable basket riding on her hip, and her hair flattened by the rain. Christopher looked around behind him for any other approaching means of rescue, but there was none. He could not avoid this meeting. Far less could he drive past Miss Prentice in his gig without offering the poor young woman assistance since they travelled in the same direction.

She accepted his help with gratitude, and after loading the basket and her damp person into the gig, Christopher took up the reins and they lurched off. Miss Prentice seemed excited and very pleased to see him, her face wreathed in smiles as she gazed up at him breathing, "Thank you, Mr. Morton!"

He had to tell her. He hoped she wouldn't cry, or create a scene. Christopher knew he must douse the girl's pretensions, and took his fence flying. "Miss Prentice," he began awkwardly, "I must speak to you on a matter of a personal nature..." Realising his words very well could sound like the prelude to an offer of marriage, he blanched white, his words caught frozen in his throat. He choked out, "Please, let me begin again..."

Miss Prentice looked at him wonderingly, and blushing profusely said, "Oh, Mr. Morton! I... I...," she stammered, holding up a hand in mild protest. "Please, you don't need to finish! I very much thank you, Mr. Morton... and I am most truly honoured..." Christopher swallowed convulsively. Miss Prentice rushed on, "I have something to say." She turned to face him squarely. "For however much I hold you in esteem, and thank you from the bottom of my heart for all the kindness you've shown me, I must tell you that... although at first I thought you... I..." Here she broke off in evident confusion, and then gushed, "Oh, Mr. Morton! I am so sorry to tell you this, but I have fallen desperately in love with Mr. Keevey!"

For several moments Christopher sat staring at her in stunned silence. Then, he began to laugh in a deluge of mixed relief and joy, for he could imagine no better outcome, no better match, for Miss Prentice than Gregory Keevey.

On a fine Sunday afternoon not long after this surprising meeting, Christopher and his mother had a small feast and toasted one another on their matchmaking endeavour. For Christopher had, that morning in church, read the first banns for the upcoming marriage of the happy couple. He had come home after the service and declared he had never felt happier to remove his boots, coat and hat, and loosen his cravat than he did that day. His mother too, had been lively. She had not fully recovered from her mystery ailment, but nor had she taken to bed again during the daytime since that day he had asked for her help in matchmaking for the Keeveys.

One fine but chilly day the following week, Christopher stood on the doorstep of the vicarage, transfixed by the pink morning light shining on the yellowing trees. He breathed deeply, inhaled, and held his breath a few moments before forcing it out between his lips, wondering at the simple delight of seeing his breath twist and float like a spirit in the air. He hurried down the steps and headed along the path to the church. A goodly number of the hired carpenters had worked yesterday on the frame for the coming stained-glass window, and he was eager to see their progress.

The pleasant, grinding sound of his solitary footfalls in the gravel was interrupted by the hoofbeats of a single horse cantering up the church road. Christopher turned to see who approached, and discovered it was a groom from Penfield House.

"The Earl has sent for you!" announced the groom, drawing up his horse. "Will you come, sir?"

"Of course! I will be there as quickly as I can." Perceiving the probable significance of the summons displayed by the urgency of the messenger, Christopher was already in motion.

When Christopher was shown into the room where the dying lord lay, he found the Earl had entirely lost the gift of speech. but he beckoned for Christopher to pull a chair near, and he shakily rested his cold, weak hand in Christopher's warm, strong one and closed his red-rimmed, watery eyes, and smiled just a little. Christopher's chest felt heavy. He had grown to care for Lord Stafford over the course of the year, and was sorry to realise that he would likely not be called upon further, but nor would he wish to see the Earl's suffering prolonged.

Lord Stafford possessed a dry and entertaining wit that Christopher would not forget, although he could not help but notice it had frequently been laced with bitterness. It seemed to him that the Earl must have achieved success that had not brought him peace. He had often wondered if his lordship had speculated and won, but at some personal expense that would gall him until his days ended. That last day may mercifully have arrived.

As Christopher sat in quiet reflection, he thought about Lord Penfield, and wondered if, or how long ago, a messenger had been dispatched to fetch him home. He hoped for the Earl's sake that the Viscount would arrive in time to say goodbye. It would be far more fitting for Lord Stafford's son to be sitting where he sat now, holding the hand of his father.

Chapter Nine

C herise went through social activities like a lady asleep, yet walking. She knew how to be coldly elegant, and she put this defence to use as often as she was able, without her mother's knowledge. Cherise, her mother and aunt were invited to card parties and luncheons now. Earlier there had been dances, but they had ceased for the year. Cherise marched through them all like an automaton, hollow on the inside, a system of gears turning, telling her to lift a spoon here, to smile there.

But upon arriving at what Cherise expected to be just another monotonous soiree, she was shaken from her unfeeling state when she discovered the subject on everybody's lips was the rapid departure from London of Lord Robert Penfield. That very afternoon word had arrived that his father had passed from this earth.

All the way back to Aunt Clara's, and as they climbed the stairs to their rooms, Lady Hamblin droned on about the Earl's death and the Hamblin responsibility in the face of it. "It would be insupportable to stay in London under such circumstances." ... and, "they would be expected at the funeral".

Cherise could not resist a cry of relief that night. Although she knew that her future was tenuous, at least she had been spared a forced promise of marriage to a stranger. She could go home and nurse her sore heart.

Early the next morning, Lady Hamblin had her sister's female servants (that could be diverted from their usual duties) collect washed clothes, fold them, and pack trunks for her and Cherise's journey home. By late morning they were loading into the carriage, and Mrs. Hamblin was sniffling discreetly into a handkerchief after having bid a hasty goodbye to her beloved sister. Cherise was pale and quiet. She was happy to be returning home, but did not wish to flaunt her ease of leave-taking when her mother obviously found it so distressing.

The long trip home was a silent one. Cherise was lost in her own thoughts and was grimly pleased that her mother, for once, shared her mood. The discomforts of distance travel only added to their downcast spirits.

When the carriage at last reached Cherrybrook and their own front door, a small swarm of servants surrounded them to carry in the luggage and escort them inside. Before the ladies had finished climbing the front steps, Lord Hamblin came out to meet them, and held out his arm to his wife. Cherise followed as he led them to the privacy of the drawing room. Once the door had been closed behind them, the questions poured from Lady Hamblin.

"When is the funeral to be held, Hamblin?" his wife inquired, stripping off her gloves. "We could not have missed it, could we have?"

"No, my dear. It is tomorrow morning. Take your rest today and recover from your journey."

The morning of the funeral dawned windy and cold. Cherise's maid, Susan, had gotten herself up well before dawn to press a heavy, black pelisse and gown for her mistress. Cherise sat silently while Susan arranged her hair. It was not the sort of event that merited any more than some curls near her cheeks and a tidy and simple bun to fit inside a velvet bonnet.

It was a grim family group that met downstairs for a small breakfast before making their way to the carriage. Few words passed between them.

Leaving the drive, the carriage turned left and Cherise looked out the window to the right, toward the path that led to the willow pond. She wondered what she would find there when she was next able to escape for a walk. She wondered what Mr. Morton had heard about her, if anything. She sat silently and faced forward. It was a certainty that she would see him shortly at the Earl's funeral, but here she stopped herself. It was inappropriate to be thinking about her own selfish concerns at this time, circumstances being what they were.

It did not take long by carriage to arrive at Wellsey. The closer they drew to the house, the more people they saw gathering and walking in family groups in the direction of the manor. The driver pulled up at Penfield, and the Hamblins descended, making their way to the heavy doors at the front of the house. Today the entry was decked in wide, black-ribboned bows, and the butler and footmen greeted them sombrely, ushering them inside.

Almost immediately she and her parents were led past the fine portrait of the youthful Earl. How elegant he would always look here upon this wall in his gilt frame. His colours would remain vibrant and lively, even though the people who had brought the breath of life to the piece were gone, both subject and painter.

Sooner than she might have wished, they passed from the gallery to what must certainly have been the study of the Earl. The room was draped in the obligatory trailing black cloth and was warmly lit with brass standing candelabras. In the centre of the room, upon a massive desk, was an embroidered, silk-covered coffin, surrounded by fragrant flowers and herbs.

The room was not crowded. The townspeople remained outside and would walk along behind the funeral carriage to the church.

Cherise lowered her head in a silent prayer but raised it quickly when she heard quick, confident steps of a man alone. It was Mr. Morton. Her breath caught in her throat as their eyes met. His expression was soft and sad. He looked away from her without a smile. Truly there was no light in this room beyond the flickering, yellow candlelight. She stared at the floor whilst listening to his quiet words of comfort and murmured greetings to each of them. All but her.

As soon Lord Penfield joined them at the striking of the hour, Mr. Morton lifted his hands and said, "On behalf of the succeeding Lord Stafford and his aunt, Lady Beaton, I welcome you today to pay your respects to the late Earl and to those who survive him in the dawn of their grief. Let each of us search our minds and find those best memories of Lord Bertram Stafford, the Earl of Wellsey. Let us search our hearts and discover what God would teach us about generosity and greatness of character as shown by the life of our departed father, brother and friend."

Mr. Morton glanced at her when he said "friend". Had it been on purpose? The brief, heartfelt eulogy continued, and when he had finished with a prayer and benediction, he dismissed the small crowd, and swept out of the room. Of course, he must. He would need to rush to the church cemetery in order to receive the body for its final rest in the family crypt.

Cherise lifted her gaze just enough to follow her parents from the room as they retraced their steps to the door. Out of the corner of her eye, she saw the young Lord Stafford lift his chin and wiggle his lower jaw about, as though he were trying on a new expression, an even more arrogant one, to match his improved title.

Outside, the wind struck her face and tugged at her hair. She squinted her eyes and looked at the drive, still alive with local citizens, dressed in their woollens, stomping their feet and clapping their gloved or mittened hands to keep away the chill. Most gazes were fixed on the elegant black funerary coach and the black-feathered, bedecked coal-black horses, who snorted in eagerness to be off with the notable burden; their nostrils dilated and heated breath opaque in the cold air. Eyes cast down, Cherise could hear a swirl of voices, scuffles of feet on pebbles and horses pawing, carriages crunching away before the procession on foot beside the coffin would begin their slow journey to the church. The air smelled of horses, woodsmoke, and fallen leaves.

She stepped up into the Hamblin carriage behind her mother. Her father would be walking alongside the Earl's casket. She leaned her head against the cold window and watched as the final touches were put on the funerary carriage, and the mourners assembled beside the coffin. At last, they were on their way.

As women outside the immediate family were considered too delicate to attend the burial, she and her mother waited inside the carriage, each with a blanket upon their laps. They sat in silence. Cherise looked resolutely out the window, avoiding conversation with her mother by looking absorbed in proper maidenly thoughts. In fact, she was hungrily taking in the view of what she could see of the vicarage and grounds.

There was the footbridge that she supposed Mr. Morton must cross several times a day. There were the herbaceous borders, now mostly wearing dusky yellow and coppery foliage. A few cold-tolerant blooms, their heads bent, quietly showed as spots of faded pink and red. The window clouded with the steam from her breath. She lifted her gloved hand and rubbed a spot of glass to peek through. She could just make out the house. She bit the inside of her cheek. She would happily step down from the overly large house where she had grown up, for this charming, large-enough home. A home with Christopher. When she felt bound for stinging tears over what could not be, she let the viewing circle on the window steam up, effectively blocking her view.

The morning after the funeral, Cherise opened her paint box and took out her letters to Mr. Morton, stowing them inside her bodice. Then she tied the ribbons on her black bonnet, threw her mantle around her shoulders, and hurried to Carter's Pond.

The willow tree branches now hung as golden strands, beautiful against the reflected blue sky in the water. She knelt down and peered into the end of the log, and felt as deeply as she dared, even taking off a glove to use her bare fingers to feel for crevices that she may have missed. She found nothing. Nothing at all. No written explanation of circumstances, no story of a new love, or a forced engagement.

A murder of crows flapped overhead, their shrill, ominous calls taunted her and added to her deepening sense of abandonment. She plunked down on her usual seat and stared up at the clear autumn sky without blinking, until tears streamed down her cheeks. What had she expected? After months filled with the excitement of a forbidden friendship, she had left Mr. Morton without a word. They had both known from the start that their differences of station would be insurmountable. Anyway, it was too late. The summer was past, and with it had flown her childish hope that something miraculous might happen to change their fate.

She traced the lines in the tree roots with her finger. Perhaps in some similarly twisted way, Christopher was being selfless. Maybe like her, he had realised that their love would devour them and give them no rest. Nothing felt better at that moment than to give herself up to crying in the nest-like solitude of the willows, away from the judgements of her mother, aunt, and listening servants. She bent forward, hugging the tree trunk, and let the past weeks of pent-up sobs wrack her body.

When she had spent her tears, she dried her eyes and slid her own letters back inside her mantle, near her heart, and trudged home. She left the fallen tree empty.

Cherise delayed entering the house, choosing instead to linger in the garden to ostensibly reacquaint herself with the dying roses. When she felt able to go inside, she walked in stealthily, stopping in front of a looking glass in the front hall to tuck in her errant hair and put her hands on her cheeks to cool the flush. She was just about to proceed up to her room, when she heard someone arrive on horseback. She waited in the hall to see who the doorman would admit. She was startled when the door was opened, and she heard a familiar voice uttering sharp commands to a groom or assistant as he hastened up the steps. In confusion, Cherise backed away and tried to fix a look of calm on her countenance, but she suspected it would be in vain. She wondered if she still looked as though she had been crying.

"Lord Stafford, Miss," said the doorman in a steady voice.

The young Lord Stafford was dressed head to toe in elegant mourning attire, but the flesh around his eyes was swollen and there was a wildness in his expression that she had never before seen.

Observing her there, he clapped his booted heels together and bowed stiffly. "Miss Hamblin. I hope I find you well?"

"Yes," lied Cherise. "I wish to tell you once more that I am sorry for your loss. I cannot begin-"

"No. I imagine you cannot," he interrupted. "Even though we have all been expecting it, it has been quite a shock. Quite a shock."

Judging by his appearance, it certainly looked to Cherise as if it had been more of a shock to Stafford than she would have supposed. How could his father's eventual death be anything but expected?"

She was moved from her internal monologue by the entrance of her father. She looked from one man to the other. For a moment, she felt like a rabbit caught in a snare. *For what could Stafford want to speak to her father about, but her? No, it could not be. So soon upon the heels of his father's passing? Even Lord Stafford could not be so unfeeling.*

As if sensing her gaze upon him, Stafford forced a strained smile.

She looked away.

"Perhaps you should offer Lord Stafford a brandy, Papa," said Cherise.

"Of course." Her father sent her a dark look. "I do not need my daughter to be so bold as to mete out strong drinks on my behalf," Without another look at her, he said, "Come, Stafford. Follow me," and the two men disappeared in the direction of her father's library.

Becoming aware of herself, Cherise realised that she was perspiring and must appear as wild as Stafford had. She unclenched her hands, which had become clammy with anxiety.

Cherise removed her boots and outdoor clothing and went upstairs to change her dress. She tried to relax in her room, telling herself that she was overwrought, and no amount of worrying would change the inevitable. But still, she could only sit a moment before succumbing to the urge to circle the room like a prowling animal. She waited in agony for her father to call for her, but he did not. Instead, after an interminable length of time, she heard the men's voices in the downstairs hall, so she slipped from her room and stood in the upstairs landing, just out of sight, and listened.

She heard her father say, "Do arrange to see me as soon as you return. I trust that if there is anything to be done, our Mr. Gaston will be able to find a way to do it. My advice to you, is not to speak to anyone about this matter. Let your lawyer and mine sort it out between them. Continue as you would have done and with luck, a legal loophole may be found."

Father's solicitor! Father was giving Lord Stafford the name of his own solicitor, but why? Cherise peeked her head around the corner in time to see Stafford stash a ribboned roll of parchment inside his cloak, and take his leave.

She darted back through her bedroom and looked out her window. Below, she watched as Lord Stafford snatched the reins of his high-strung horse from the hands of a groom, and vaulted himself up into the saddle while the big horse reared up, side-stepping with the bit in its frothing mouth. The powerful animal was off like an arrow as soon as Stafford gave it rein to go.

Cherise rushed down the stairs in an effort to reach her father before he closed the door to his study. "Father!" She called out to him. He had his back to her, but he turned to face her when he heard her call out.

She saw that her father looked neither angry nor happy. He looked bewildered.

Forgetting better manners, she asked, "What is it? What has happened? Lord Stafford did not come here about me, did he?" she inquired nervously.

Lord Hamblin's brows creased like oak bark. "No. That was not why he came. I cannot tell you the precise reason for his visit. Suffice it to say, that the old Earl's will has an unexpected peculiarity. Always secretive until the very end. I should have been prepared for some such disclosure, but I confess I am caught off guard. I am sorry, m'dear. I can tell you no more than that.

"Go up to your room and have a rest." His brows creased again as he searched her face and, perhaps for the first time, saw distress etched there. "Yes. Have yourself a rest."

A few days after Lord Stafford's hasty interview with her father, Cherise had accompanied her mother to Wellsey, and now sat in the best parlour of Mrs. Terrence. She wondered to herself how her mother justified being so intimate a friend of a woman who was married to a gentleman with no title, who had bought his way into the gentle class. Then, she supposed that, in her mother's estimation, having a *friend* below your station, and a *husband* below your station, were two *very* different things.

She sat as usual in the soft chair near the front window and looked out at the street. There were a surprising number of cheerful-looking persons dressed in their Sunday best, walking in the direction of St. Joseph's Church.

"And dear Cherise..." She turned when she heard herself addressed. "You have no news to share from your London stay?" Mrs. Terrence asked.

"Not the sort that would interest you, I think. I saw a Roman Art exhibition that pleased me, and Mother was kind enough to take me to three musicales and several architectural tours." Cherise gave her mother's friend a soft smile and went back to looking out the window.

Mrs. Terrence blinked slowly, a frozen smile pinned to her face, and turned back to cast a sympathetic look at Mrs. Hamblin as if to say *"far too blue"*.

Behind Cherise, the older women had moved onto the topic that had prompted the visit: the mysterious will of the late Earl. Cherise listened but did not engage in the conversation, having nothing to say on the subject.

In a conspiratorial tone, Mrs. Terrence was telling her mother that there must have been something unusual in the will, because there were murmurings amongst the household staff at Penfield, that the new Lord Stafford had "scarcely been sober two hours together since the reading of it". Perhaps there was a portion that he could not touch, Mrs. Terrence speculated, or could not until some sort of condition was met. "Well," Mrs. Terrence went on, "whatever it was has caused the young Earl to behave recklessly! He disappeared for a handful of days, and now has installed some of his more rakish associates as house guests at Penfield, and the crowd of them is now carrying on in a way that does not at all respect propriety for a house in mourning."

When there was a break in the ladies' stream of conversation, Cherise asked, "Is there a celebration today of some kind?" Her eyes widened and she looked to Mrs. Terrence for confirmation, "It is not the unveiling ceremony of the new church window, is it? I have not missed it?"

Mrs. Terrence set down her teacup and bustled to the window to peer out. "Oh no. The window ceremony is to be on All Saints' Day. Good gracious! I had forgotten about the windows ... No, the small crowd you see must be for a wedding. A widowed farmer named Keevey is marrying the eldest Prentice girl, Miss Eliza, today. She is the one I wrote to you about during your stay in London. Do you recall it? Apparently, she had an infatuation with Mr. Morton, and had got it into her head and, shamefully, on her tongue, that he intended to offer for her! Well, he was so attentive to her welfare, you know. But anyone could see that the whole situation was ridiculous. A wealthy vicar is still vastly above the reach of a mere country female, no matter how good-hearted and sweet, and our Mr. Morton *is* a gentleman."

Mrs. Terrence soon changed topics, having no idea of the effect of her words upon her young guest, who felt suddenly ill. Cherise asked her hostess, almost in a whisper, "Forgive me for interrupting, Mrs. Terrence, but when was it discovered that the news you had written to us in London about was merely idle gossip?"

Mrs. Terrence paused with her teacup part way to her lips and said thoughtfully, "I suppose it became clear when the first banns were read for Mr. Keevey and Miss Prentice." Here the woman sensed tension in the room and looked to her friend, "Oh dear me, did I not write to tell you, Augusta?"

"No," replied Lady Hamblin simply. She was carefully watching Cherise, who appeared to be taken ill, for her daughter's chest was rising and falling at an alarming rate, as though she were taking too many shallow breaths too quickly.

Cherise was aware that Mrs. Terrence went prattling on, but about what, she did not comprehend. The blood was rushing in her ears and she heard nothing. Instead, she put all her effort into breathing, and hoped the tightness of her corset, combined with the shock, did not cause her to faint.

Mercifully soon, Cherise's mother finished her tea and stood, signalling the end of their tete-a-tete, and when they had said goodbye to Mrs. Terrence, and been seen into their carriage, Lady Hamblin did not force Cherise to speak, allowing her daughter to keep her thoughts to herself.

Once they arrived, and Lady Hamblin had changed out of her cloak, hat, and visiting clothes, Cherise watched fearfully as her mother stalked off to Lord Hamblin's study, knocked forcefully on the door, and was admitted into that private sanctum.

Chapter Ten

His mother seemed to be slipping away, bit by bit, since the Earl's death; or so Christopher feared.

He had just come from her room, and now stood with his cravat still untied, and the top buttons of his shirt undone, staring out the window at the pouring rain. It had rained ceaselessly, making the whole of the day a sort of dismal twilight. Somewhere in the gloom, the sun was setting. He ran his fingers through his hair in distraction and took a deep breath.

He could not understand what was wrong with his mother. She had been the picture of robust health when they had first arrived in Wellsey. She had come willingly, eagerly. She had wanted him to make a home here. Last winter and spring they had enjoyed countless, long country walks on fine days, and she had had no trouble keeping pace with him.

Yes, she had complained of frequent megrims in the summer, but she had rallied for the latter part, only to have taken to her bed again now. Why, the day before yesterday had been the Keeveys' wedding, with blessedly fine weather, and his mother had cried off attending, even after all her sacrifice to bring the marriage about. Would she be well enough, have *will* enough, to attend the unveiling of the church's stained glass window? Invitations had been posted. The ceremony on All Saints' Day was only eight days from now.

Thunder clapped somewhere in the distance. Christopher watched as a fresh bank of clouds rolled closer. He drummed his fingers on the sill as he leaned against the window frame.

There was something pressing upon his mother's soul; something she would not, or could not tell him. Maybe the time was coming when that would change. He jammed his fisted hands deep into his pockets, and took another turn about the room. Was he imagining the connection between the old Lord Stafford's death and his mother's depressed state? Might Lord Stafford have been his father? It was too ridiculous, and yet... He had assumed that he was a by-blow son of a peer or wealthy merchant ever since the age when he could be sensible of his situation. What other condition would explain the financial support that he and his mother had always received? And, if his father had truly died years ago, why had her family and his father's family not been more attentive to the widow and son? He had been reared in wealthy isolation, the distant, yet enduring family connection with the Earl would explain that perfectly. Besides, had his mother not shivered and gone pale at Lord Penfield's dinner party, when they had stood together beneath the full-length portrait of the Earl? Had she not been too weak to attend the funeral? He took a few slower turns around the perimeter of the room and stopped again at the window. It was unthinkable that he could lose his mother when she had no acknowledged disease! But as soon as the thought had crossed his mind, he pinched his eyes shut - for his own chest throbbed as though it had been torn, reminding him that sorrow and loss were themselves a kind of sickness, but of the heart.

He looked down at his hand. What if his own hand, which had held the Earl's during his last breaths, *had* been the hand of a son?

Somehow, it felt right. His mind reeled. If this were true, would it change anything?

Even if he could not yet unburden his mind, and share the significance of his suspicions with Cherise, he needed to see her; to demonstrate the strength of his regard. He could no longer sit idly by and watch her marry Lord Robert Stafford. If I am indeed *any* son of my father, I would speak. I have gained nothing by my silence. The time has come for me to be forthright for the small chance that she may consider me, as I stand, her most devoted admirer. I have no choice but to leave the rest to fate.

Frustration coursed through his body. Desperate for action, he had to *do* something. He looked out again at the pounding rain and thunderous clouds, and thumped his fist against the wall. He strode into the hall and pulled on his boots and hat, threw open the door and rushed headlong into the downpour.

He started off blindly in the direction of Cherrybrook. The storm outside was nothing to that which raged inside him.

When he was beyond the last house of Wellsey, he grinned recklessly, and tore off his hat, heedless of the water streaming down his face. He began running, and did not stop until he reached the Artist's Folly. Evening and rain had swallowed the willows by the time he reached them, but still he paused, glancing in their direction. Today, with his turbulent thoughts and a lover's impatience, he would pass the trysting spot and advance directly to Lord Hamblin's front door.

In a moment, he was crossing the road and jumping the stile that connected the road with the Hamblins' estate.

He emptied the rainwater from inside his hat before knocking. He was sure he looked like a poor soul straight from Bedlam, but he did care.

Loudly rapping on the door, Christopher nodded to the footman who opened it.

"I am Mr. Morton," he said. He paused for a moment to catch his breath. "I desire to speak with Miss Hamblin and her father." He could feel rain dripping from his lips as he spoke. He brushed them away with a wet sleeve.

The footman pulled the door wide open to allow Christopher to pass (stepping aside quickly to avoid getting wet in the process), when from the darkness behind them came a loud cry, and the grinding sound of a carriage being driven too quickly up the drive. Christopher turned toward the shouts. Perhaps like himself, the footman suspected an emergency, for he left Christopher and hurried into the house, calling for Lord Hamblin.

Christopher held the door ajar in his hand whilst shielding his eyes from the raindrops. He could see the carriage now, and strained to identify it by its mud-splattered crest or an identifier of some kind, perhaps horses that he could recognise.

Before he could distinguish anything, the carriage door burst open and two gentlemen leapt out onto the gravel, and a third man came pounding up the drive on a powerful hunter. This third man (whom Christopher recognised from Penfield's dinner party) dismounted nearly before the great horse had stopped. The horse was steaming as the cold rain hit the heat of its body. It jumped around, taking heaving breaths through its dilated nostrils. The man let the reins fall and ran to the carriage door, bellowing over his back to Christopher, "Open the door, sir! We have an injured man here!" The same man turned and shouted vaguely in the direction of the Hamblin stable yard, "Someone! John Coachman! Bring us a fresh horse- we need to ride for a surgeon immediately!"

The Hamblin footman had returned with the lord of the house on his heels. Christopher let go of the door and ran down the steps three at a time until he was at the carriage. Without thinking, he crowded in. He was as athletic as any of the others and reached in to grab an arm of the injured man, helping gently, but quickly, to drag the gentleman forward and out the door of the carriage. The man was covered in blood and, as soon as they had lifted him completely from the floor of the compartment, his head lolled back alarmingly. It was Lord Robert. Christopher froze, immobile in shock, and his stomach lurched. Beside him a voice barked, "Someone support his head!" Christopher looked away from the grisly sight, instead focusing his energy on working with the others to carry the young earl through the rain and up the steps.

Once inside the house, he heard a woman scream. Christopher glanced up. He saw Lady Hamblin clap her hand over her mouth in horror and rush for her husband's arms. Cherise stood, supporting herself with the newel post of the hall stairway. He had no time to interpret her expression. There was a call from outside and he jumped for the door.

In the drive, one groom held the carriage pair, which bumped and jostled about in agitation, and a second groom held the big riding horse which had its tail lifted and was prancing about, whilst the groom tried to get it walking in tight circles in a vain effort to calm it.

Christopher heard a bang from the stable and the sounds of hurried movement and not a moment later, a third groom came running out with a dry, saddled horse and a questioning look on his face.

"Wait!" shouted Christopher, holding up his hand to the groom. "I will get someone from the house!" He ran back up the steps and opened the door, "A horse is ready! Who is going for the surgeon?"

All pairs of eyes fixed on him at once and he suddenly became aware that the room had gone quiet and all action stilled. Then Cherise, her face deadly pale, dropped to the floor with a thud.

He rushed to her at the same time that Lady Hamblin did.

"Susan!" screamed Cherise's mother shrilly, and from somewhere in the house, he heard the clap of women's shoes hurrying across the hard floor, and a maid came bursting into the hall and ran to the side of her fainted mistress.

As Christopher instinctively reached out his hand to move Cherise's hair that covered her mouth, he realised that he was dripping blood and rainwater on the floor, and saw that his hand was stained crimson. He stopped himself and stood, taking a step backward, struggling to absorb the altered situation.

He turned to the huddled group of men who knelt next to Stafford's prostrate form on the floor. The one he recognised, Lord Nye (the man's name came to him) had red eyes, and he blinked tears away as he glanced up at Christopher and said bitterly, "No surgeon can save him. We'll be needing the undertaker."

"I... I will send a groom, then." Christopher hesitated and raised an eyebrow at Lord Hamblin, seeking permission. Hamblin nodded and Christopher crossed the yard again in great strides. He found the groom standing where he had left him, holding a ready horse, whilst the others were occupied with the spooked hunter and the restless carriage horses.

"I regret to say that Lord Stafford is beyond the aid of a surgeon," said Morton, "please locate the undertaker and bring him.

"The rest of you carry on. I have no idea how long his lordship's friends will be inside."

Christopher started to go up the steps again, but he stopped midway, turned, and slowly walked back down. When he'd reached the bottom, he gazed at the front of the house. He wanted to push his hands into his pockets, but he remembered in time that they were covered with blood. Instead, he let them fall uselessly to his sides. The messenger had been dispatched, and the other grooms were unhitching the carriage team. He could hear another fellow speaking in a low voice to Stafford or Lord Nye's dragon of a horse, deep inside the stable yard.

He was no longer needed. He would go home. His macabre presence could bring no comfort to the Hamblins and there was nothing more to be said or done that night.

His return home was much slower than his run to the Hamblins' had been. His energy was drained. And whilst the thunder had abated, the darkness and rain persisted. As water stung his straining eyes, he realised that he had forgotten his hat at the Hamblins'. Not that it signified.

He tried to think about what had just occurred and feel something. *Anything.* Guilt, sorrow, pity, anything at all. But he felt nothing.

He closed his eyes and slowed his breathing. He listened to the wind in the leaves and the rain slapping into puddles. When he opened his eyes again, and looked down, he caught sight of his hands. They were stiff with cold. He flexed them and peered at his palms. The blood had been partially washed away by the rain and the rubbing of the woollen cuffs of his greatcoat. Maybe some of it had been absorbed by his own skin. It was strange. Perhaps it was not a bad thing to feel nothing. He hoped that Cherise and her mother were staying in their rooms until Stafford was taken out, and the hall washed clean of the blood and mud.

For the remainder of his solitary walk, Christopher listened and watched, resigned to a silent heart.

It was in this same state of emptiness that he arrived home. He explained to the anxious servants what tragedy had struck Lord Stafford, assuring them that he, himself, was in no way injured, despite the alarming stains.

"I am, however, in need of a bath, and my clothing needs attention if it is not already too late," he said. A manservant practically tore the boots from his feet, rushing off toward the back of the house with them, promising to clean away the blood. Barefoot, Christopher proceeded upstairs and once having attained his room, he stripped down piece by piece, until he was handing the last of his garments around the edge of the door to a waiting servant.

After washing his face, arms, and hands thoroughly in hot water, he dressed in a suit of dry clothes and went in search of his mother.

Seeing a light still shone under his mother's door, he knocked softly, and pushed the door open.

"Christopher?" She spoke his name like a question. She still rested against a small mound of colourful pillows. She set down the book she'd been reading and motioned for him to close the door. He crossed the room and sat down in the chair beside her bed.

He leaned forward with his elbows on his knees, folded his hands under his chin, and smiled grimly. Her gaze searched his face. "What has happened? Your hair is wet."

Carefully expunging unnecessary details, Christopher laid out the terrible events of the evening, and his mother cried into a handkerchief without attempting to speak until her eyes dried on their own. When finally she looked up, she appeared weary, but a curious relief also showed in her face.

She began to push the blankets aside, and said more to herself, he thought, than to him, "I do not care a piece about the money, but I do care about your reputation and your prospects."

Christopher knit his brows, "I beg your pardon. Mother, have you not been attending to me? For I do not know -" but before he could finish his sentence or reach forward to stop her, Mrs. Morton had dropped her legs over the side of the bed and crossed the room to her bureau. She slid open the bottom drawer, taking out a small, cloth bag that looked like a large, folded lace handkerchief, and slipped her hand inside one end of it. She pulled out a small, sealed envelope and handed it to Christopher.

She climbed back into her bed, and leaned back wearily. She smiled at him, her eyes moist with emotion as she said, "Open it. I did not think I would be alive to see you read this letter. I did not expect the death of Lord Penfield nor would I wish to take joy in it, but I have longed to be able to tell you who you really are."

"I believe I already know," Christopher replied gently. He broke the wax seal and opened the single sheet, spreading it upon his knee.

He read:

If you should read this letter, Christopher Harwick Stafford (called Morton), it means that I, Bertram Robert Stafford, and your mother, Beatrice Harwick-Johnson (called Morton) or your younger half-brother, Robert Lewis Stafford, are now deceased.

You are to offer this letter to my solicitor, Mister Joshua Havers Esq. or as a second, Mister Carlton Jennings of Cherrybrook. In my records and last will and testament, it will have been discovered that large sums from my estate and enterprises have gone to the bank account of Mrs. Beatrice H.J. 'Morton', my beloved mistress, beginning in the year of Our Lord, one thousand, eight hundred and thirteen (1813). I have done my best to divide my estate to honour my legal wife and mother of my heir, Mrs. Mariah Wilton Stafford. I was a faithful husband from the beginning of our marriage until the last.

The entirety of the Wilton family monies is to be given to her son, as well as my name and title. If, at the time of my expected death, my legal heir has not convinced me of his fitness to receive the whole of my estate and living (minus the ongoing and permanent payments to Mr. Christopher Morton and his mother Beatrice Morton), then the estate and living shall be divided between my sons as determined and made legal by my final will and testament.

As a personal addendum, I hope that I have given you, Christopher Stafford Morton, every advantage that was within my power to give a first son born in such circumstances.

This is signed and dated: Lord Bertram Robert Stafford 1832

When he had finished reading, he handed it back to his mother and she smiled a little.

"Was he good to you, Mother?"

"He was," she whispered. "You and Lord Robert both shared a bit of him. You have his appreciation for art and a well-turned phrase." She looked down in quiet reflection before continuing. "However, when the Earl was young, he was a handsome coxcomb and perhaps overly confident. Fortunately for me, he loved me truly and, even though he was forced to marry at his parents' bidding, he would not let you and me fall into poverty. He said goodbye to us... such a difficult time. I feared for his reason. But he made me sign and swear I would not reveal the truth to you until he, his wife, and any of their surviving heirs were gone. He became very wealthy because he took risks where others would not, and he succeeded in nearly everything he invested in; well beyond expectation. Intelligence of your education and progress was delivered to him by way of his solicitor. I knew his end must be near when he sent for you."

They sat together in comfortable silence for a moment, and Christopher told her how he had held his father's hand during his last moments.

"I believe that he must have been taken with you," said his mother, "proud of you, from the first time he laid eyes on you last autumn. In a way, perhaps you have redeemed him," Mrs. Morton said wonderingly. She sank back against the pillows again. "I think I should like to be alone for a while now, Christopher," she said quietly. "You needn't worry. I feel sure that I will recover my strength." She looked into his eyes and placed a hand to her heart. "This secret has eaten through my heart and my conscience these past many months. Of all the temptations I have had to face, standing silently by and watching you fall in love with a woman as beautiful, and smart, and worthy of you as Miss Hamblin, and not being able to reveal your identity because there was still the Viscount to consider, was the most difficult thing I have had to endure. I will not speak ill of Lord Penfield, but I think that, had I respected him more, it would not have taken so much charity and selflessness on my part to keep my promise to your father."

He looked up slowly, "I am glad you did not tell me. I think I should have disappointed myself with jealousy and anger. As it is, I feel guilty. For I live while he does not." He said in sotto voce, "may he rest in peace."

Chapter Eleven

When Cherise regained consciousness, she found herself in her own bed with the curtains drawn. Susan was sitting next to her in a soft chair with some mending to occupy her. She set it off to the side when she saw Cherise looking at her.

"Was it real, Susan?"

Susan nodded, wide-eyed. "You were very brave, miss." Cherise turned away. "I was not. I fainted."

Susan replied with a dismissive sniff, "You fainted because your stays were too tight. I shan't lace you up that tightly again unless we are in Town."

Cherise smiled at that as she sat up and let her feet fall off the side of the bed.

"My orders were to keep you to your bed," said Susan. "Are you certain you feel strong enough to be sitting up, miss?"

"That is what I am ascertaining," Cherise flicked her ankles and flexed her feet.

"I think I am well enough to put on my slippers and talk to my father. Do you know if he is still at home? Or if- if any of the other men remain?"

"Your father is in his study. He shut himself in there quite some time ago." Susan hesitated, "All the men have left." She eyed Cherise carefully before adding, "and the... the disorder has been put to rights."

Cherise nodded, "Thank you, Susan. Please bring me my flannel dressing gown."

Once she had been helped into the comforting garment, Cherise padded out the door and down the stairs. Her teeth started to chatter when she reached the bottom step where she had witnessed Lord Stafford's injuries and subsequent death. She hoped someday that she could forget the sight of it. Shuddering, she turned aside and made her way to her father's study.

"Come in," called her father when she knocked.

She entered quickly, closing the door behind her, and when she turned around, she was surprised to see that her mother was in the room as well. Lady Hamblin was curled up in a large chair near the fireplace, like a much younger woman might be supposed to do. Cherise nodded and bobbed a curtsey, but did not sit down.

Both her father and mother watched her and seemed to be waiting for her to speak. Cherise cleared her throat before speaking, and when she did, her voice sounded shrill and far away somehow.

"I just woke up. I-I asked Susan if everything that happened today really did happen, and she said it did, just as I saw it. I think I fainted before-before comprehending-" she was struggling to find the words, which now came tumbling out, "the Viscount... that is, Lord Stafford, did in fact die, did he not?"

Her mother looked at the fire and her father nodded, frowning as he did so.

Cherise took a step closer. "Father, may I know now what it was that Lord Stafford came to see you about?"

Lord Hamblin looked at his wife, and Cherise followed his gaze. Lady Hamblin nodded stiffly for him to speak.

"He was seeking my advice on a legal matter. It seems that the Earl had written a rather unusual will, one with addendums ... and letters held by others to make it complete and readable. There was no question as to Lord Stafford's having inherited the honorarium of his father, but the estate entails were open to contest." He paused as if he were waiting for her sluggish brain to catch up. She frowned, not understanding what it was that he was expecting her to suddenly comprehend on her own. Finally, he went on.

"The will revealed the fact that Lord Robert has an elder half-brother, an illegitimate one-"

"Stop! Oh, stop for a moment," begged Lady Hamblin. Then she turned to Cherise and said, "Sit down, child." Cherise's stomach churned oddly and she crossed her arms as she sat down in a large, leather chair opposite her mother.

Lord Hamblin took a deep breath, and just as he was about to speak, Cherise's eyes grew round. She had the feeling that she knew what he was about to say.

"-Mr. Morton is that brother. The Earl had provided for him and his mother covertly all these years. Not even Morton himself knew who his father was."

Cherise was stunned. It was several moments before she could find her voice. "What will happen now?"

Her father rocked on his heels and put his hands behind his back. "The will must be read again in the light of all that has just occurred, and the missing addendums gathered from Mrs. Morton and a second, distant solicitor whom Lord Stafford used to take care of the matter of his elder son and mistress." He paused and looked up at the ceiling. "I imagine when all is said and done, Mr. Morton will inherit all, including the title of earl. He is the only remaining issue of his father. And he is acknowledged."

"I see," was all Cherise said. She sat still for a time, staring into the blue flames of the fire and blinking back tears of hopeful incredulity. As if in a dream, she rose and quietly left the room.

After she had gone, her father said to her mother, "Do you know, my dear, I have never seen Cherise look so haunted as she has since you returned from London. And then to have had such a day as *this*, and for her to leave this room with all the radiance of an angel. What has happened to her?"

"She is in love, Hamblin."

"With the vicar?"

His wife nodded thoughtfully and slowly lifted her eyes to meet his gaze, "He is not merely a vicar anymore, after all."

The following day, the Hamblins attended regular Sunday services at their own parish in Cherrybrook, and returned home to await news from the coroner.

With the testimony of Lord Robert Stafford's friends, there was no question but that the cause of death had been a fall from his horse.

According to their congruent accounts, Lord Robert had been in emotional distress and drank heavily before riding out into the storm. Lord Nye tried to bring him back in, but he would not listen. They rode behind him and saw him get tossed violently from his horse when a deer startled his mount. His lordship's friends then hailed down a carriage and asked the owner to take their horses back to Penfield, whilst they carried him by carriage to the nearest estate they could find, Lord and Lady Hamblins'.

Upon hearing this final report, and learning that the funeral for young Lord Stafford was to be in three days' time, Cherise spent the rest of that afternoon in her room with a ribbon-tied bundle of letters upon the corner of her writing desk, her pen, ink, and blotter in front of her, trying to draft a letter to Mr. Morton. The dustbin near her feet was already half full of crumpled rejected beginnings.

She had spent hours sitting with her feet pulled up, hugging her knees and looking out of the window, puzzling over what Mr. Morton had come for on the day of the accident. Was it really only a day and a half ago? Had he been out riding with Stafford's friends? That was not possible. Christopher was not cut from the same cloth as those others, and he had never mentioned any partiality for hunting or horses, so how was it that he had come bursting through the door? Had he been coming to see her? To talk to her father?

Perhaps that was the first thing to ask in her letter.

"Friend,

I hardly know where to begin..."

When she arrived at Carter's Pond later that day, she felt vaguely disappointed not to find Mr. Morton present, but then, she realised, with a family funeral to plan, as well as a window to unveil, he could not sit idly waiting. She tied her velvet bonnet on more tightly and pulled her matching black velvet muffler about her neck. She lifted her heavy skirts and found the driest places to walk as she continued down to the fallen tree.

She sat down upon the log, removed a kid glove and put her hand in the crevice to feel around. There! Wedged deep inside the end of the log was a folded letter.

Her heart pounded painfully as she pulled it out of hiding and eagerly moved to sit in her usual place. She took off her second glove and unfolded the letter with her trembling hands. A small shaped paper form fell out as she opened the letter, and she reached down to catch the shape up and study it. It looked like a folded bird, about the size of a matchbox. She held it in her closed fist as she hungrily read the message. How beloved his handwriting had become, and how she had missed it.

"Friend,

I have a long way to go before I can fold a thousand cranes like this one, but according to orizuru (crane) legend, if I do, either my soul will be carried to paradise or one wish will be granted me. To me, the rewards seem much the same. If I am in paradise, it follows logically that you must certainly be there, and if I have but one wish granted me, it would be to spend the remainder of my days with you.

I trust that very soon we may meet face to face.

Perhaps I assume too much?

I was on my way to ask for you when Lord Stafford was carried to the house. There was every likelihood that, had I succeeded in pressing my suit with your father then, I would have been sent out the door, and perhaps he and I would be sporting black eyes today! Now I have reason to hope my offer will be looked upon favourably. If you have not heard the news, if you have any doubt about my allusions, please ask Mrs. T.

Yours forever and a day,

CM"

Cherise laughed and cried as she read his letter several times over.

Chapter Twelve

Agentle, clear autumn day came on the back of a full moon. It was All Saints' Day and Cherise and her parents had been handed out of their family carriage at the front of Saint Joseph's Church.

She stood for a minute, wanting to commit to memory the picture of the swaying green and yellow grasses against the deeper greens, browns, and golden oranges of the leaves in the sunshine. She closed her eyes to steady her breathing and listened. There was a delicate strand of a melody drifting from the open doors of the old stone church. She heard the rustle of her mother's taffeta gown and the crunch of the leaves under her mother and father's boots coming abreast of her, and she opened her eyes again and smiled.

It was a moment long-awaited, and such a sight it was! As they entered the church, Cherise gasped as her gaze seized instantly upon the brilliant colours of the window, really three windows, before her. The day was sunny, and it set off to advantage the radiant richness of the glass, and the fineness of the composition. The piece was a triptych, a three-part depiction of the Holy Family out-of-doors, against an azure sky. The left panel revealed a kneeling angel with his head up-turned rapturously towards the centre panel. Above the angel, in the middle of the tallest arched window, was the Christ Child, seated on His Mother's lap. Finally, Saint Joseph stood under the branches of a fruiting olive tree in the right panel. Restful sheep, tiny plants, delicate flowers and reddish rocks were at the foreground of each section.

Transfixed by the beauty of it, Cherise stood still until her mother gently took her by the arm and led her to an empty pew. Once seated, Cherise made a discreet search of the rest of the clerical platform. The altar table was laid out with small, unlit candles, with draperies of white cloth and wreaths of rosemary, chrysanthemums, and grape vines. Her attention was captured only momentarily by the sway of the choir singers and the fluid movements of the violinists. Divine as their music was, they were not what she sought. *Ah, there.*

Seated modestly off in the far-left corner was Mr. Morton. As soon as Cherise saw him, her mouth went dry. Even from this distance, she knew he was looking at her. She saw Mrs. Morton turn her head a little to look behind her, and when she saw Cherise, her eyes lit up warmly.

The church continued to fill, and the air was punctuated with exclamations of surprise and admiration. When the music came to a close, Mr. Morton stood and walked forward, coming down on the same level as the seated crowd. He held his arms out wide, "Welcome, each of you! It is my privilege to present this window to the people of our town. May it bring solace and hope to the hearts of each of us who is here today. And not only our hearts, but those of our children," here he smiled at a pair of fidgeting children near the front, "and our children's children.

"This particular theme from the life of our Lord is especially pertinent and precious when unexpectedly following the deaths of the cornerstones of Wellsey. The Holy Family and what they represent should comfort us in times of joy and sorrow, for it is a reminder of the love that binds families across generations. Death cannot extinguish love.

"As the musicians perform "For All the Saints", we will light these first candles in celebration of all the saints who have gone before us and attained their rest. This evening and tomorrow, please say a prayer in memory of Lord Bertram Stafford and Lord Robert Stafford, and for each soul that you have lost that was dear. Let no one be forgotten.

"It is not a time for improper grief or despair but rather, remembering. Let us rejoice that they have apprehended Heaven."

Mr. Morton turned and invited the musicians to take up their instruments and the hymn began, clear, and joyous, and swelling.

As each name of a now absent relative or friend was called out, a candle was lit.

Cherise saw heads bow as candles flickered, a discreet embrace here, and there a hand held.

As the hymn played on, Cherise and many others in the parish joined their voices with the choir's. A stray sunbeam came shining through St. Joseph's hand which was placed over his heart. Cherise could not help but feel that it was a special benediction from fathers to sons. Her eyes misted as she watched Mr. Morton. She wondered what he must be feeling now that he knew who his father had been.

At the end of the service, Mr. Morton walked to the back of the nave, inviting the congregation to rise and move closer to the windows, better to appreciate the details if they so desired.

Surprisingly, Lord Hamblin hung back for a time with Lady Hamblin and Cherise waiting behind him. When he was ready, he stepped into an aisle and walked to meet Mr. Morton, extending his hand. He shifted his hat in his hand. "Mr. Morton," he said, "You and your mother are still able to join us for dinner this evening?"

Mr. Morton bowed his head, "Yes, sir. We are looking forward to it," his eyes flickered to Cherise's face.

Lord Hamblin's moustache rose on one side as he said, "I see you are. At five o'clock then."

Everything slows down when one is in love, decided Cherise while dressing for dinner that afternoon. She had shut herself in her room with Susan, and had spent the greater part of an hour trying on dark gowns. She was on her second time through, when Susan exclaimed, "Miss, do you remember that black and burgundy fine-striped silk that had a torn undersleeve? It is hanging in the laundry, waiting to be pressed. I can see that it's done and bring it to you."

Susan bustled away and soon came back with the gown draped over her arm. The deep red and black was perfect. As she checked the way the drape of the skirt fell over her mistress's hips, Susan said admiringly, "You look just radiant, miss," she smiled.

"Thank you," said Cherise. "I will wear this one. Please help me lace up... not too tightly, mind you," she added, her eyes twinkling.

"Aye! You are bound to have trouble breathing, the vicar is *that* handsome! You'll be the envy of every young woman for miles about here, now. And to think that he might be an earl after all! It is almost too much to take in."

Cherise smiled, warmly. Susan was probably correct. She would be the envy of many.

Mr. and Mrs. Morton had no such sartorial difficulties. They both wore mourning black, although Mrs. Morton had two black caps to choose between. Christopher had his beaver hat.

"Are you nervous?" asked Mrs. Morton.

Christopher chuckled in response. "Should I be? Hamblin's altered manner and invitation for this evening has gone a long way to convince me that, when everything is settled, and if my condition is pleasing, he will approve my offer for his daughter." He grinned mischievously, "Do you know? It has been a long time since I have feared anything half so much as Lord Hamblin's opinion!"

They bundled up in cloak and greatcoat, with large, woven mufflers and gloves. Turning to the hall table, they took up their lanterns for later, and were then ready to leave.

The well-sprung carriage rocked along on the road, not badly, for the wind was not strong, but there had been some damage to the road from the previous storm, especially where it ran low, nearest to creeks and riverbeds.

Christopher, who was watching out the window, said, "I cannot believe all that has happened in this past year." He glanced at his mother. "I first set eyes on this lovely place in the autumn, this very stretch of road, and I still think it lovely."

"You will be happy to travel, though?"

"Naturally! I think my first trip will be a wedding tour." He smiled broadly and stretched out his legs in mock arrogance, but then his expression softened and became more serious. "It will take some time to put our affairs in order, and I shouldn't want anyone to feel rushed. I think perhaps I will talk to Lord Hamblin about his nephew for the church. I could use a curate. There will be urgent matters at Penfield, and I will need to spend increasing amounts of time looking after concerns there."

"To think that you will be in your father's house! I never dreamed it possible that you would be known for who you are, but it was not so bad a thing, really. I prefer you as the unselfish man you are. And," she added after a moment's thought, "who is to say but that your life, as it has been, did not make you thus?" She quoted with a smile, "The grapes that struggle the most grow the sweetest."

Christopher reached over and gave his mother's hand a reassuring squeeze, then settled back to see what he could of the rich, golden world that was passing by his carriage window.

When they arrived, Christopher unfolded his tall frame as he stepped from the carriage. Reaching back in, he took up the lanterns and, holding tight his mother's gloved hand, helped her alite. She didn't require much assistance, for now she was recovering her strength, and each day they found she had more stamina, and her prior spirit of youthfulness was returning.

They paused for a moment, looking up the stairs. The Hamblin house was an imposing, blockish home, with strong lines and only modest embellishments. Although typically it had an elegant but cold aspect, this evening there were large baskets of harvest flowers and candles lit, even though it was not yet fully dark.

The footmen had been expecting them, and anticipated their knock. They bowed and opened the door wide. Christopher's heart made a jump, not of nervousness, but of joy. His senses were nearly overcome by the delicious scent of a fine venison, and fruit pies, as well as the cinnamon, ginger, and allspice of baked soul cakes. It was surprisingly warm in the house. He could hear the tapping of soft boots and shoes on the hardwood and stone floors. All this he absorbed in a second, and these pleasant gifts to his senses were nothing compared to the vision of Cherise who stood before him in the centre of the hall like a shade-grown flower.

She was wearing a finely-striped, dark dress with a full skirt that pulled in tightly at her waist and hugged her curves, leaving her beautiful neckline and a face as pale as moonlight. There was something to be said for the new gown styles. She was smiling and her lips were rosy pink, he found himself wondering how long he would have to wait to finally kiss those lips. Her smile grew wider, and he imagined that he must look as foolish as a schoolboy. She raised an eyebrow and her lips parted. Somehow, he managed to look away from her when her father and mother stepped forward. How long they had been standing there, he had no idea, so enraptured had he been. He hoped that he had not been rude.

He bowed politely. "Lord Hamblin, Lady Hamblin, thank you for inviting us this evening. We are most grateful for your generosity and kindness." Mrs. Morton also moved forward and added her appreciation.

"Do not apologise, Morton. I am afraid it has been rather late in coming," Lord Hamblin's moustache rose up on one side, which probably indicated a smile. He clapped his hands together and rubbed them. "Let us take your coats," he beckoned a footman to come help the guests remove their outer wraps. "Ah! I see you have brought lanterns and candles for tonight. Excellent."

Lord and Lady Hamblin were a stiff, formal couple, but Christopher hoped that with time, they would soften towards him. He and his mother's health were inquired about, there was mention made of the shocking death of Lord Robert (as they were all gathered in the same hall, it could hardly be avoided), and then they proceeded into the dining room to enjoy the dinner courses that smelled so tantalising.

After the last plate had been cleared away, and the ladies had retired to the drawing room, Lord Hamblin invited Christopher to his study for a drink, and wasted no time before delving into the younger man's affairs in a friendly, but direct manner. He told him about the visit he had received from the Viscount, and that he himself had already seen the will, or at least the portion that Lord Penfield had brought with him. He asked about lawyers, and what Christopher was currently doing to fix his interests as heir. Apparently satisfied with the answers, it was Lord Hamblin who brought up the subject of Cherise.

"It has been brought to my attention that my daughter has a... decided affection for you. Whilst I do not believe the popular insistence that romantic love is a necessary component of a marriage arrangement, I am a fortunate man in that I married at the design of my parents, but found my wife easy to care for. That is to say," clearing his throat with a mild cough, "we have a genuine affection for one another that goes beyond obligation." Lord Hamblin looked down as he swirled his last bit of spirits around in the tiny glass. "My daughter is wilful and has an artistic temperament.... likes art, books, that sort of thing. She told me that your knowledge of one another has been nearly entirely through correspondence."

"Yes, sir."

"You know then, that she is as I have described?"

"And more, yes," smiled Christopher.

"I confess I feel better about giving her into the hand of a husband whom she respects. Once you are installed as Earl of Wellsey, you will have made the matter of getting her married appropriately, and with her cooperation, excessively easy." Here Lord Hamblin sighed, lifted his glass and winked at Christopher. "I am grateful to you for that."

"Sir, there is something," started Christopher. "Beginning next week, I will be seeing appointments and beginning the preliminaries of moving to Penfield House. The household staff has only just been told about the more surprising contents of the will. Fortunately, I am rather well acquainted with most people in the house, and I flatter myself that I am liked and will be welcomed." He took a deep breath and let it out slowly. "But doubtlessly, there will be some who will be ready to find fault with my upbringing and stubborn independence." He grinned and then slowly his mouth relaxed as he became more serious. "Besides, the world is changing, and I want to be sure that Penfield and its resources are used in ways that benefit the people of Wellsey. With all of this to manage and more to come, I find I am in immediate need of a curate. If your nephew is still in need of a position, please have him apply to me at once."

Lord Hamblin looked pleased. "Of course. Thank you for your kind consideration. And if you are ever in need of advice, you will find me a willing counsellor. Anytime you have need of me, you know where to find me."

Lord Hamblin puffed out his cheeks and looked a little discomfited by his own words. "Yes, well..."

Christopher finished his drink, took a step forward and set the empty glass on the tray. "Thank you, sir. For everything."

Hamblin studied him with one eye squinted and said, "I think you will fill your father's shoes admirably. Now, let us re-join the ladies."

The men left the study and entered the drawing room. It was warm, with a cheerful fire crackling in the fireplace, and a row of elegant, lit candles on a table. Cherise was bent forward, looking out of the window, candlelight illuminating her face. "I see more coming down the walk!"

She smiled over her shoulder adoringly as Christopher crossed the room to her.

"Children asking for soul cakes?" he inquired huskily. He was surprised he could speak at all. To have Cherise so near...

"Yes! Our kitchen staff was busy baking all day, and the cakes smell wonderfully, do they not? Mrs. Silts is in charge of passing them out, and is sitting with a basketful just inside the front door." She turned to those in the room behind her and blushed, catching Christopher's rapt gaze. "Are we ready to walk to the churchyard?"

"I believe we are," said her father agreeably. "Morton and I have warmed our throats with brandy and unless I am very much mistaken, he would like nothing more than to walk with a lantern on one arm and you, my dear Cherise, on the other."

"Hamblin!" said Cherise's mother severely. "You mustn't say such things." Her rebuke was quite robbed of its significance, however, as her next comment was, "Well, go on, child. Have Mr. Morton help you with your cloak."

Christopher turned to his mother, "Will you join us?"

"I think not. I will wait here for you. This fire is very friendly," she smiled. "Instead, I would like to hand out a few cakes if it is alright with you, Lady Hamblin?"

"Certainly," their hostess responded. "You must do what pleases you best. I will ask Silts, our housekeeper, to set you up with a comfortable chair near her own in the hall."

Cherise stood tall and lifted her skirts a little from the floor and swept toward the open door of the drawing. She walked very near Christopher as she did so, and gave him a look that set his heart thrumming, and made him feel as if he had just drunk a second brandy in one swallow. "Will you help me with my coat, Mr. Morton?" she prompted mischievously, her eyes twinkling.

He followed her into the hall and pulled down her heavy, fur-trimmed pelisse from the hook, and held it over his arm for a moment, swallowing hard as he asked, motioning in the vague direction of his own collar bone, "Miss Hamblin, will you be warm enough... here?" He hoped he sounded less overcome than he felt at the prospect of his knuckles grazing her bare neck and shoulders.

She took a step closer to him and replied softly, "I will be plenty warm, thank you." She turned her back to him while looking over her shoulder with all the mystique of one of Titian's models, her gaze never leaving his.

Christopher shook out the garment and gently pulled it around her reverentially, savouring her nearness.

Her parents entered the room and called for their wraps, and Christopher stepped backwards a polite distance from their daughter.

Soon all four of them were bundled up in their heavy black silks, velvet, and wool. Each took up a lighted lantern and went out the door and down the steps. With a smile and an understanding wink, Lord Hamblin took his wife's hand and placed it firmly on his arm, and they set off in front of Christopher and Cherise at a fast pace.

Christopher stood still for a moment, watching the backs of the lord and lady in the dim evening light.

"It is not far," said Cherise, her breath curling in the cold night air. She huddled closer to him. When he looked down at her, he saw that she smiled up at him charmingly.

"When you smile at me like that I cannot think." He laughed softly, and then added, "It's not far you say? I was just wishing the walk were a long one."

She chuckled and blinked again. "Well, we do not have to walk quickly."

Christopher's brow creased, "Are you cold?"

Cherise lifted a dark eyebrow, then she relaxed her mouth, and looked intently at Christopher's arm. "I think we ought to proceed, Mr. Morton. Even if we decide to be slow about it, we are already quite left behind." With a roguish smile, she threaded her arm through his, very tightly, and pressed herself against him saying, "This is much better. Now I am warm enough, thank you."

Christopher beamed down at her, and the two walked down the drive to the main road. They stayed a distance back from her parents so that they could speak freely. Up ahead, and indeed all around, they could see little bobbing candles and lantern lights emerging from neighbouring houses forming a dotted, golden strand as others also made their way from house to house, or up the winding lane to the cemetery. The night air smelled pleasantly of the smoke from warming fires and damp leaves, as well as the melting wax of the tallow candles in their lanterns.

After they had talked about how horrible the day of Lord Penfield's death had been for them, and the contrition that each had felt once they realised they were likely to benefit by it, they moved on to a review of Cherise's stay in London and what had happened between Christopher and the now Mr. Keevey and Mrs. Keevey. When Cherise asked what he and her father had discussed in the study, Christopher stopped suddenly, and held Cherise tightly by the hand.

"Before another minute goes by, Miss Hamblin, I want to be sure that we are in complete accord. You can have no doubt of what my wishes are in regards to you. Only one question remains, and I believe it is more of a formality at this juncture, but..." She looked up at him with a trusting gaze. "Will you be my wife?" He set the lantern down so that he could take one of her hands in both of his. He searched her eyes and face, wanting to memorise her beauty, and read the love in her expression so that, come what may, he would always possess this moment.

She looked down, and he saw by her cheeks that she smiled, and she said, "I have dreamed of this moment, even when I believed that it could not be, and here we are..." Her voice was tender and nearly a whisper in the wind by the end. "Yes," she breathed, "with all my heart." She looked up at Christopher with tears in her eyes and a brilliant smile that began in the corners and ended with a mischievous grin. "-Here we are. Alone. In the dark."

Christopher laughed softly, "Why, my dear Lady," he said in mock astonishment, "are you asking me to kiss you?" Before she could answer, he pried her gloved fingers from the lantern she was holding, and set it on the ground next to them. With a throaty chuckle, he pulled her into his arms, gently enfolding her at first, and then pulled her in closer, kissing her slowly, searching her mouth with his, curiously. He had closed his eyes, concentrating on the new sensations exploding inside him, but slowly he opened his eyes and pulled himself reluctantly away from Cherise. He watched her dark eyes flutter open; her red lips still parted alluringly. He glanced with a regretful smile in the direction of her parents, and with a hand still pressed into the small of her back, he lifted his other hand to his mouth and pulled the leather glove off with his teeth and let it fall between them. With bare fingers he traced a line over her lips, and lightly pushed up on her chin to close her mouth.

She lifted a questioning eyebrow and bit the inside of her cheek, "Was that... enjoyable?"

"You teasing female, you know it was," he said with a crooked smile, "But I should not be allowed another intoxicating sip like that for a while, for it will make our engagement feel like the sweetest torture and an eternity of the worst kind." He laughed ruefully as he fetched his fallen glove, and then said very seriously, "Thank you, Cherise. You've made me a very happy man."

He stooped and picked up their lights. After handing a lantern to Cherise, he took up the other, and with Cherise snuggled in close on his arm, they set off once more on the road before them.

As they got closer to the churchyard, they were joined by dozens of other couples and families, slow-moving widows and widowers, and running children. Ahead of them, they could see Cherise's parents just entering the wrought iron gate. It was an eerie, but beautiful sight, with warm light illuminating the statuary, headstones and family tombs. For, during All Hallowtide, the cemetery looked and felt very much like a large hall, with welcoming places set for the living and the dead. There was little wind, but a smattering of small, dry leaves drifted down like snow, flickering dark against the orange candlelight.

Christopher paused at the gate, but Cherise gently pulled on his arm, leading him through the crowd to stand beside Lord and Lady Hamblin. Amidst the hum of murmured prayers and quiet conversations, they lit candles before the stone statue of Saint Joseph, patron saint of fathers and families. The collective glow of many candles illuminated the mossy stone ledge and the faces of the others gathered nearby.

When they had finished, the Hamblins and Christopher slowly threaded their way back in the direction of the entrance, stopping now and again to wish a friend or acquaintance a joyous All Saints' Day.

Some children recklessly darted past, their clumsily-carved turnip lanterns dangling precariously. A few townspeople or parents admonished them for their rudeness, but the laughing youngsters ran on, impervious to correction.

No one objected to Cherise and Christopher walking arm in arm. Nor was a word spoken when they dropped behind once again, lost in their own whispered conversation about their plans for the future.

The echoes of evening revellers' voices were mostly behind them now, as they walked along the dark road. When they saw the lights in the windows of the Hamblin house, and the dark silhouettes of Lord and Lady Hamblin walking up the drive, the young lovers grew quiet, savouring the sweetness of being alone, side by side.

In this moment of contented silence, Christopher saw Cherise smile.

"What is it, my love?" he asked.

She looked down briefly and then up at him, her face aglow. "It was you who gave the church the painting and even the windows, was it not?"

Christopher nodded slowly.

"You must have a great deal of money."

Christopher hesitated a moment before answering, "I do."

They walked a few silent steps ahead, and then he added, "It was not enough, though."

"It wasn't?" Cherise asked in confusion, looking up quickly. "I do not mark you as an avaricious man, not in the least."

"I do not believe I am. To me, money is a means to an end; to take care of the necessities of my life and the lives of those I am to care for, to aid the suffering of my fellows and give them hope in any way I can; through art, for example. Naturally, that takes very little effort for someone in my position to say, and I do wrong by claiming that I am not greedy, when I have always had more than enough of anything money could provide. I have not been injured by want, and, in a certain light, I am ashamed of that." They walked a few steps more and he went on. "In other words, I feel as though I am extraordinarily privileged without deserving it. The fortune of birth and the unhappy events that have led to this serendipitous day, were completely beyond my power to control."

"Then, what is it that you lacked?" asked Cherise, mystified.

Christopher looked down into her lifted eyes with such a look of tenderness, that Cherise couldn't breath for a moment. He picked up her hand and lightly kissed her fingertips, and whispered, "Why, only you, of course, my dearest love," he beamed.

Cherise clung to his arm, feeling overcome by the deep emotions that his loving words evoked.

When they got back to the house, Mrs. Morton was waiting with cakes she had reserved for them, still warm. Their festive fragrance filled the hall. In high spirits, the chilly foursome removed their overcoats, hats and mufflers, and everyone returned to the drawing room. Standing in front of the fireplace, with a glowing fire at their backs, Mr. Morton and Miss Hamblin announced their engagement, and were gratified by the sincerity of the congratulations offered them. Lord Hamblin proposed a toast, and each drank to the happiness of their future together.

When Christopher stepped into the carriage that night, after a lingering goodbye to Miss Hamblin, he banged his head into the door frame. The impact was hard enough to make an audible sound and his hat fell off. The driver turned quickly to see what had happened. "You all right, sir?"

"I am," said Christopher, stooping to retrieve the hat. He then tried again, this time successfully landing in the seat across from his mother. He set his hat on the seat beside him and smoothed back his hair. He saw his mother smile despite the darkness.

"I thought perhaps you just lost your head," she commented, her eyes dancing.

"At this present moment, I do not believe I would notice," he replied.

The carriage began to move out of the yard and into the drive. Mr. Morton and his mother leaned against the sidewalls of the carriage, and watched the soft lights of the Hamblin house disappear from view.

"To lose my head would be one thing, but losing my heart is quite another. I am very content."

The End

Thank you for reading!

D id you enjoy Christopher and Cherise's love story?
If so, please leave me a positive review. It helps me as an author immensely, and it helps other readers find new, good books!

Discover more books by Charlotte, and sign up to her mailing list and get a digital copy of "Creatures of Habit" FREE, when you visit: https://charlottebrothersauthor.com

Already have Book One? Charlotte's mailing list friends will be the first to get new free goodies.

Any questions or comments? Please email: charlotte@charlottebr othersauthor.com

Look for her on your favorite online book place: BookBub, Goodreads, Facebook, Amazon and more.

Also By

"A Year in Cherrybrook' is a book series of sweet late Regency/early Victorian era romances. Four light-hearted, character-driven love stories take place in spring, summer, fall and winter in or around the fictitious English country village of Cherrybrook. They may be read in order or as stand-alone stories.

CREATURES OF HABIT | Book One: Spring
The Boy-Next-Door Returns...
Can unconventional Eugenia Merritt and Lieutenant Lawrence Trellaway stand against their well-meaning parents' matchmaking attempts? https://books2read.com/u/mY87LW

A FAIR-WEATHER FRIEND | Book Two: Summer
Is the wrong brother the right man?
Miss Marian Lyle knows what to do with a column of figures or a garment to sew, but a charming newcomer has her in a muddle!
https://books2read.com/u/mg1gqX

A BIRD IN THE HAND | Book Three: Autumn

Art, Fate, and Forbidden Love

A handsome new vicar and the local baron's daughter: art brought them together, but will fate pull them apart?

TIME WILL TELL | Book Four: Winter

Matchmaking gone wrong

Mrs. Lavinia Fitzroy is just the woman to find widowed Dr. Rafe Reynolds a wife. She's audacious, well-connected and entirely uninterested in marriage for herself...

About the Author

C harlotte Brothers lives in Michigan (USA), with her delightful family, beloved pets, and a busy bird feeder. She does her best to write heartfelt stories about memorable characters with a dash of humor and playful prose.

Manufactured by Amazon.ca
Bolton, ON

29135762R00104